THE LAST
OF THE
STORYTELLERS

BRINTON FARRAND

authorHOUSE®

AuthorHouse™
1663 Liberty Drive
Bloomington, IN 47403
www.authorhouse.com
Phone: 833-262-8899

This is a work of fiction. All of the characters, names, incidents,
organizations, and dialogue in this novel are either the products
of the author's imagination or are used fictitiously.

Published by AuthorHouse 09/28/2020

ISBN: 978-1-6655-0002-9 (sc)
ISBN: 978-1-6655-0003-6 (e)

Print information available on the last page.

Interior Image Credit: Title page: Brinton Farrand

This book is printed on acid-free paper.

CONTENTS

Acknowledgments ix

NEW BEGINNINGS

Chapter 1   Torture 1

Chapter 2   Kelly's Rescue 7

Chapter 3   In the Beginning...11

Chapter 4   More Stories..15

Chapter 5   Outsiders 19

Chapter 6   Robots 21

Chapter 7   Back in the Collective 23

Chapter 8   The Controller and the Woman in Black..... 27

Chapter 9   Billy and Kelly Leave 31

Chapter 10   The Gift 35

Chapter 11   Jake Allen 41

Chapter 12   Sid Finch 45

HUNTING SEASON

Chapter 13 Talon Explores 49
Chapter 14 The Silencer Finds Help 53
Chapter 15 The Killing 57
Chapter 16 Brucie finds Muddville 63
Chapter 17 Sid meets Shoop 67
Chapter 18 The Keys Brothers 73
Chapter 19 Secrets Told 77
Chapter 20 The Warning 81
Chapter 21 The Crime 85
Chapter 22 Cody's Rescue 93

THE ADVENTURE BEGINS

Chapter 23 Kim's Assignment 99
Chapter 24 Taking Care of Problems 107
Chapter 25 Kim 111
Chapter 26 The Celebration 115
Chapter 27 A Meeting with Jake Allen 119
Chapter 28 Jake Allen's Busy Day 123
Chapter 29 A Night at Pat's 131
Chapter 30 The Fight 137
Chapter 31 Shoop's House 143
Chapter 32 Kim and Manon Return to Muddville.....147
Chapter 33 The Library 153

A NEW TEAM

Chapter 34 The Silencer and Talon Team Up 159
Chapter 35 Dan Shoop's Home...................................163

Chapter 36 Manon Goes Hunting 169
Chapter 37 The Hidden Treasure...............................173
Chapter 38 Kim Meets Sid...179
Chapter 39 Everyone Heads West 185
Chapter 40 The Westward Trip Continues.................189
Chapter 41 The Inn 195
Chapter 42 The Silencer Captures Billy......................199
Chapter 43 The Last Day... 203
Chapter 44 Manon and Billy..................................... 207
Chapter 45 The Battle with Talon (Kim narrates) 209
Chapter 46 Recovery..213
Chapter 47 Life at the Inn...215
Chapter 48 The Future...219
Chapter 49 Big Plans... 223

About the Author.. 225

ACKNOWLEDGMENTS

To write this book I had a lot of help and inspiration. This is in memory of one of my biggest influences in my life, Dan Shoop. He was one of the best history teachers at Carmel High School, along with being a great educator, and may have directed me into my teaching career.

I must mention all my friends that I called in to proof my book and give me their opinions and ask questions. My many thanks to Pam Taber, Lisa Goble and Brandy Sawyer for questioning me on character content. Markeus Farrand raked me over the coals about the Collective and how it worked which made me rewrite the book to its current form. I thank you.

Needing the help of the younger generation's mind, I constantly asked my daughter Jackie for advice. Last, but not least, my wife Claire spent countless hours editing this book which I'm sure she didn't count on when this venture started. My thanks to both of you.

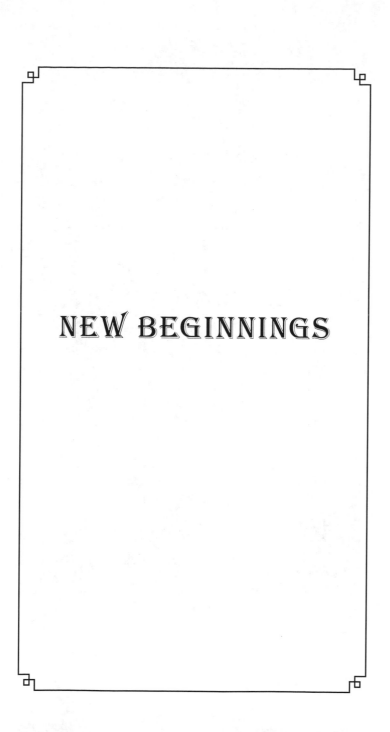

NEW BEGINNINGS

Kelly Sitting in Her Cell

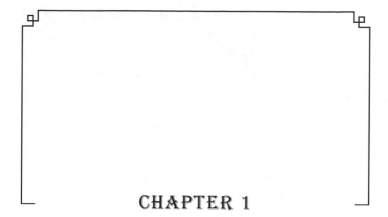

CHAPTER 1

TORTURE

K elly Schneider had been isolated for two weeks. Her prison was dark and confined; the cell she had been placed in was no home. The results of her isolation in captivity began with headaches and dizziness. Her captors messed with her mind, regulating the temperatures; one day extremely cold and the next boiling hot. The worst part for her was sitting in a pool of sweat, and then feeling the sweat freezing to her skin the next unbearable moment. Food. Food, what there was of it, was rotten. Starving, her body was in shock and she began to lose weight. It did not help that the guards randomly pounded on the door to interrupt any chance of sleep. Kelly's mind was a nightmare. Phantom monsters haunted her every moment, whether she was awake or asleep. Her only saving thoughts were thoughts of her family. She missed her father the most. It was he who had guided her through school and all the tests of the Collective.

The door banged open. Desperate for something to drink, she looked up. Bart Archer grinned down at his prisoner. He was the Silencer. That was the title of his position and what most people knew him by. This was his favorite part of the job, interrogation.

"Well Miss Schneider are you ready to talk? Give me some names? Details of the outside world?"

Kelly just stared at the man. *Everyone in the Collective feared him. He was the second most powerful man in the Collective. People did not survive after his interrogation.*

"Everything you know! Now!" He screamed.

Kelly dropped her head and began to sob. *Betray all her friends, how could she?* "No!" she stammered, staring up at the Silencer.

The Silencer laughed.

Kelly blurted out, "I am saying nothing. Kill me now." *That sounded braver than she really was.*

Looking at Kelly with a gleam in his eye, he said "Death? Death would be too good for a traitor to the Collective." Turning, the Silencer slammed the door. Kelly could hear the man march away. The click of his heels on the concrete floor faded away.

The Collective had many buildings; storage facilities is what they really were. Kelly was being housed in the back corner of one such building.

Kelly dozed off and she began dreaming. She was drowning in a muddy river. Her arms and legs were not moving fast enough to get her to safety. The harder she tried, the more futile it got. She began to panic as the water started to pull her under. She screamed. That scream woke her up and she looked around.

At that very moment, the Silencer opened the door, "Good you're up. On your feet."

Kelly's legs wobbled as she stood. A guard grabbed her roughly by the arm.

"Bring her along and follow me." The Silencer led the way to a small room. A chair for Kelly sat in the middle of this new cell. "Put her there and tie her down."

Kelly sat weak and in shock as the man tied her wrists and ankles to the chair. The ropes were tight and cut into her skin.

The door opened and a lady in a black uniform walked in, pulling her hood down. She looked at the prisoner. Two female assistants entered after the lady. They too wore black uniforms, the standard uniform of the Collective security forces.

Bart Archer turned around. "Go get Kim Schneider and bring her here."

"Me?" The Lady in Black seemed irritated "Why don't you do it yourself?"

Archer growled, "Now!"

The Lady in Black almost hissed as she left the room.

Kim Schneider was Kelly's younger sister. It had been early March when Kelly had attempted to sneak back into the Collective. Kim had tried to warn Kelly of the danger she was getting into, but as she confronted Kelly, Archer and his men had appeared. Archer then assumed that Kim was in the process of arresting Kelly herself. That assumption made Kim a decorated hero of the Collective.

Kim walked into the room and looked around. Her face was calm, yet inside her mind was spinning. *What were they doing to Kelly?* Looking over at the Lady in Black, she saw only anger. *She must be jealous of my promotion* Kim thought. Kim then looked at the two behind the Lady in Black; Manon, the first assistant and Alice the second assistant. Manon and Kim had been pitted against each other many times in their training. She was dangerous. Alice just stood there with an evil grin, as though she knew something Kim did not.

Archer turned to the group. "You three go tell the Controller that we have the traitor and soon we will have the information we need. Commander Schneider will stay here and help with the interrogation."

The Lady in Black stomped her foot, "Commander? She's a rookie."

The Silencer stiffened, "Go now!"

The three turned and left. Storming away, Kim heard, "That fucking bitch!"

Kim turned her attention to her sister. She was but a mere shell of herself, having lost a lot of weight. Kelly was tied to the chair, sobbing.

"One last chance." Archer said smiling.

Kim looked at her sister. Tears ran down Kelly's face. She was nothing but skin and bones.

"My answer is No." Kelly shook her head.

Archer went to the desk drawer. "Well, let's try this." Approaching Kelly, he said, "Hold her tight." Each guard took hold of a wrist preventing any movement from their prisoner. Then grabbing Kelly's fingernail with a pliers, without warning, he yanked the whole nail out. Blood flew. Kelly sat stunned. It took a minute for the pain to register in her brain.

She screamed.

With stunning quickness Archer drove a hammer into the bloody finger, rocketing sheer pain through Kelly's body.

Blackness enveloped Kelly and she passed out.

Archer stepped away, looking at Kim. "Wake her up! Call me back in when she's awake."

Kim stood there staring at her sister. *What could she do? The Silencer could kill her. Could kill her whole family if she disobeyed.* Leaning over her sister, Kim lightly shook Kelly. "Kelly wake up. Kelly. Kelly wake up."

Kelly looked up into Kim's eyes. Tears ran down her face and her mouth trembled. "Tell them I love them. Tell Mom and Dad I love them."

Kim nodded. She waited several moments and then walking over to the door, she waved the Silencer back in.

Smiling at Kim the Silencer said, "See that wasn't so hard."

It had been a test. He was testing her loyalty Kim thought.

The questions came again "Who have you been working with? Who got you in and out of the Collective?"

Kim gritted her teeth and shut her mouth.

Another nail was pulled out, but this time he let her look at it as the pain soaked in. Then raising the hammer, it fell harder this time on the bloody fingers. Standing there admiring his work, he then threw a devastating punch to her left eye. Kelly slumped in the chair, her hand a bloody mess,

"I'm getting tired of this. Wake her again."

Kim began to cry once the door was shut and she was alone with her sister. She woke Kelly. "I'm sorry Sis."

Kelly tried a smile. "It's not your fault, it's all mine."

Kim dropped her head and opened the door, calling the Silencer in.

Walking in, he said "Are you ready to talk?"

Kelly nodded yes.

The Silencer beamed, "In the face of pain there are no heroes. First question, what are the people like out there?"

Kelly answered, "They are just like us." She hesitated, then it all came flooding out. "They have newspapers and there's a history teacher writing a book about the History of the World."

The Silencer was getting excited. "Give me your contact!"

Kelly began to cry again, and the Silencer reached for his pliers.

"Wait!" she sobbed. "His name is Billy. He got me in and out of the Collective. I have told you everything, now let me go."

The Silencer laughed, "It is not that simple; you are a traitor to the Collective." Turning to Kim he said, "Go tell the Controller that we have what we want."

Kim left the room looking back at her sister, maybe for the last time.

Kelly was silent. *She had never thought about death before, yet here it was.*

BOOM! An explosion rocked the building. The Silencer sprinted out of the room towards the explosion.

Kelly looked up. *What now?*

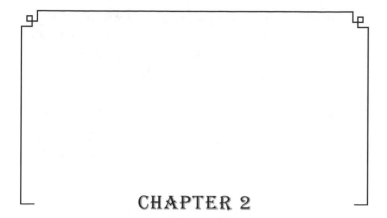

CHAPTER 2

KELLY'S RESCUE

Men of the security force were sprinting towards the explosion. The Silencer raced after them. Everyone's focus was on what had happened. The two guards waited beside Kelly.

The door to Kelly's cell flew open. A big man with reddish hair walked into the room. Grinning, he said "Fellas it's a great day to be alive." Before the closest guard knew it, a jack hammer of a right hand swung and knocked him out with one punch. The big man looked at the second guard. "Now you can go down like your friend here or you can run after your buddies."

The man's eyes widened with fear and he sprinted out of the room. Jake Allen laughed and looked down at Kelly. "Let me help you out of this chair." Untying Kelly, he lifted her up and carried her out of the room and through a nearby door. Outside it was a cloudy, fifty-four degrees. Jake handed

Kelly to an Indian. "Take her to safety! I will go help with the fight." Billy was the Indian that had befriended Kelly. He nodded and quickly headed off, supporting Kelly.

The fight was not much of a fight as neither side had many people. They were not ready for anything dramatic. Jake and Billy had organized a few farmers for the distraction, but an all-out fight was not what they were prepared for. It ended up a standoff. Only one man of the Collective was wounded. Both sides retreated slowly as the smoke from the explosion dispersed.

Several hours later that day, Bart Archer stood in front of the Controller of the Collective. "Let me get this straight, you had the traitor and then you lost her. Truth be told it wasn't you who caught the traitor, it was Kim Schneider."

Archer stammered, "Well sir, it really wasn't her, it was our scientists' tracking system."

The Controller laughed, "Nonsense! Where were your scientists when the outsiders broke into my building and where were your security forces?"

The Silencer stammered, "Well, well…"

The Controller continued, "Your job now is to fix the hole in my building and to upgrade the security forces watching the building. Do you think you can handle that?"

"Yes sir. Will the Collective learn about this attack on us?"

The Controller stood up, "Absolutely not. To master the people, we must control everything that they learn so that the people will have no opportunity but to learn what we want them to. Elimination of the free thinking. Do you not understand the ways of the Collective?"

The Silencer, seeing that he had made the Controller

mad, straightened. "Yes, sir I understand. Permission to leave, sir."

"Dismissed!"

"Yes sir."

Kelly had been taken to a friend of Billy's; a man named Dan Shoop. Billy looked at Kelly, "Are you going to be okay?"

Nodding yes, Kelly asked, "Will he come out after me?"

His response was, "I don't know. I am going to leave you with Dan. You will be safe. I am going out scouting just to make sure we weren't followed. Then I am going to watch the building for a few days."

Kelly nodded.

Dan looked at Billy as he left, "Be careful, the Collective will be out hunting."

Back in the Collective, Kim sat in her apartment trembling. What had she seen? Torture; a terrible torture of her sister. To make matters worse, she could tell no one or it would mean death to her and her family.

Kelly woke up slowly the next morning. Looking around the cabin she saw Shoop reading in a rocking chair.

Smiling at her, he got up saying "You okay?"

Kelly looked at her bandaged hand. "I'm a bit stiff and my cheek hurts."

Dan patted her on the shoulder. "It will take a good week for things to heal physically. Mentally, well that could take a long time. You were talking a lot in your dreams last night. Well, more like screaming."

Kelly dropped her head. "I'm so sorry."

"For what? It's not your fault that the Collective did that to you."

Kelly stammered, "I told them about you and your history book. I told them about Billy."

Dan turned towards the kitchen. "We figured that they would get it out of you. Shoot, I think they would get that out of anybody. Want any breakfast? Toast? Eggs?"

Kelly sat up. "Toast would be fine. Well come to think about it, I am hungry. Eggs would be great."

Dan began to cook breakfast, looking over his shoulder. "You can wash up in that other room if you like. I laid out some fresh clothes for you. Probably won't fit but they'll be clean."

Stiff and aching all over she looked at the mirror. The Silencer must have hit her with more than his bare fist. Her eyebrow was a matted mess of blood. She hung her head and tried to get rid of the memory of that awful man. Cleaning up was a slow process as her hands shook constantly.

A little while later Kelly walked out, fresh, and clean.

"Better?"

"Better!"

They sat down at the table where Dan had outdone himself, making bacon and eggs, toast, and muffins. He sat there in silence, watching her eat. She gulped down the whole glass of water. It was the best thing she had ever tasted. Her second glass she savored even more, letting the cool liquid surround her tongue and cool her throat.

Looking up at Dan. "I was part of the Collective, but how did they get started? How did they end up this way?"

Dan slowly said, "That's complicated. I will have to tell you several stories to answer that."

Kelly looked at the historian. "Well, you said Billy would be gone for days and that I need time to heal. We have time."

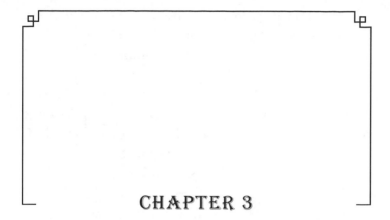

CHAPTER 3

IN THE BEGINNING

"**Y**ou are right, we do have time." Dan smiled. "To begin with, the Collective is a virtual world created by the billions and billions of people. There was a time long, long ago when the Collective was just a dream by some immensely powerful people. These elite people controlled the world behind the scenes of the politicians."

"Did they want something with the use of that power?" Kelly asked.

Dan responded, "Power gets power, there's nothing else behind it. To stay in power, they need the population to be controllable. This had been a long slow process."

He stopped, letting what he said sink in. He continued. "You see, mankind made advancements."

"In what way?" Kelly asked.

Looking over at Kelly, "Well, their education was like yours. Really just like what you have experienced in the

Collective. Their technology advanced. They had things like cars that could drive them around. Planes that flew. There were machines for everything imaginable."

Kelly's eyes widened.

Continuing, "They used a machine called a computer for their science and research." Holding up a little plastic stick. "This was called a flash drive. It could hold all the memories of the computer or an individual."

"How did you get that?" Kelly asked.

Dan was amused, "Well, some artifacts like this one were passed down through my family lines long, long ago."

"Where is your family?" Kelly quizzed.

Dan looked out the window, "Sadly all gone. I'm the last Shoop."

"I'm sorry." Kelly said.

Dan shrugged, "It is what it is." Pausing. "Out of all their advancements came a thing called AI - Artificial Intelligence. It could be taught to do things for people. Play games like chess and win against humans. AI took people's jobs. You see, it was cheaper and faster than humans. The scientists created robots. They were mechanized people. Starting out they were used to watch and take care of children and the elderly. The good was that it helped people, but the bad was it became far too constricting."

"How so?" Kelly asked.

Answering, "Consider this. You have a dog, and instead of letting him run free we put him in a cage. Now he is safe from harm and he has food. Do you think he is happy?"

Kelly flashed back to her time in the cell, "No."

Getting excited, "Exactly. Then it started. The people rebelled against the robots and artificial intelligence. At the same time, something even bigger happened. A virus. A worldwide pandemic. Both events showed the glaring difference between the rich and the poor. The haves and the have nots."

Kelly mulled over in her mind all that she had heard. "I know something about fear. What did they do?"

Dan continued, "Here is where it gets interesting. The powerful people I told you about saw their chance. The Collective at that point went from being an idea to something physical." Shoop pulled a sign out to show her and read it aloud.

> "If we come together, we can succeed.
> Together we are strong.
> Join the Collective and be strong."

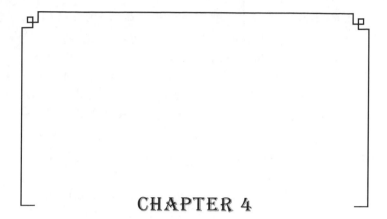

CHAPTER 4

MORE STORIES

The week was moving along quickly for Kelly, but the nights were not. The Silencer continued to appear in her dreams, and the memories of her sister made her cry. *Would she ever see her again, or even her family?*

One day at lunch Kelly asked Dan "So all those people joined the Collective. How did the people out here get here?"

Dan stood up and walked over to a bookshelf. "I have found many diaries through all of my research." He opened a journal from Kevin Sanders and began to read.

"March 24: Schools are closing. My children will have to be educated online at home."

Shoop looked up. "That's the computer thing I told you about. Kevin states here that he doesn't have the money to buy a better computer for his kids." Dan shook his head. "His last line here is. 'What can I do?'"

Flipping through the journal. "Here. March 31: The town

is on lock down. No one can leave their house. Businesses are closed. I lost my job. How will I feed my family?"

Shoop looked up, "People were getting desperate. This is not the only case I have found. There are many diaries like this. You see, the government is making people stay at home to protect them." Looking back at the journal. "April 8: The news keeps telling us to be afraid." Skimming the page. "Ah, here's what I was looking for. Kevin writes 'I heard a bit of good news today. There is a new group out there. They are called the Collective and they say they can fix everything.'"

"So, the Collective is offering the people safety?" Kelly inquired.

"And much, much more." Shoop explained. "April 15: I went down to the Collective Office today. They took my name down and the names of my family. Very friendly people. I am going to take some time to think about joining the Collective. They guaranteed safety from the virus for my whole family and a job. My family would be equal with everyone in the Collective. Should I join?"

"Last entry. April 18: We have decided to join the Collective. There is nothing out here for us. We will enter the Collective tomorrow. God be with us."

Shoop closed the book. "You see how easy it was for the Collective."

Kelly looked up at Shoop. "What about the people that didn't join?"

"Well, as the Collective became bigger and stronger, they began using propaganda. At the very end I have read stories of them hunting people down and forcing them to join. This was a long time ago. You really can't blame this Kevin fellow for joining. Think about your experience with the Collective. They gave you the rules by which you had to play. They watched over you both night and day. Your life was controlled. Your freedom was a joke."

Kelly shook her head, "I didn't even understand that until I came out here."

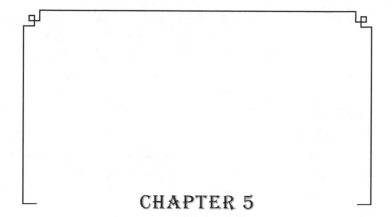

CHAPTER 5

OUTSIDERS

The next day Kelly asked, "Do you have any diaries of the Outsiders?"

"A few." Came the answer. "A lot less than those that joined. You see, only one in ten didn't join." Digging around in an old desk drawer he pulled out a stack of crumpled papers. "Ah, yes, here we go."

Reading, "Bart F. writes March 25: first day of lockdown. Schools closed. Churches closed."

"March 26: The whole world is on lockdown."

"April 1: It seems to me that the government is promoting fear to the people. Am I the only one that doesn't trust the government?"

Looking a Kelly, "You see, not all the people are reacting the same way."

"April 10: More fear, more propaganda."

"April 11: I went down to the market today. The lady

behind the counter said it would be the last day they will be open. She and her family were joining the Collective. I bought more food than I needed. It will be hard to find food from now on. I think a man followed me home."

Shoop looked at Kelly. "Can you feel the Collective closing in?"

"April 12: A woman from the Collective knocked on our door today. I turned her away. I get the feeling that she will be back. We have decided to leave for my brother's house tonight when it gets dark. It will be safe with him way out in the country. God be with us."

Shoop sat down. "There you have it. Many joined, and those few that didn't went into hiding. Both groups became absorbed in their own survival and forgot about each other. Mind you, this took maybe seven or eight generations. I'd say two hundred years. The Collective had no need for the material things in the outside world. The outsiders hid and quit using all technology for fear of it being traced. Over the next three generations, all advancements and improvements were forgotten. Really a clean slate for all. Now the Controller's main fear is that there will be a grass roots movement out here against the Collective.

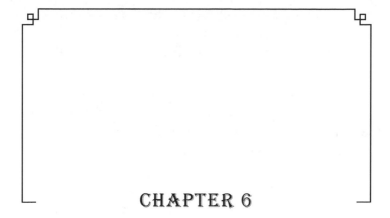

CHAPTER 6

ROBOTS

"My last question I think." Kelly grinned.

Dan chuckled, "I'm a teacher, I'm used to questions. What is it?"

Kelly sat down for more stories, "What happened to the robots?"

Shoop walked back to his books, "Well, that's hard to say. In several cases the people revolted against the robots and destroyed them. It was quite a backlash against something that the people thought was too controlling. The people felt threatened by them. There were some strict churches that believed the robots were the Devil's work. All I know is that many were destroyed. Then, after the Collective was organized the robots were forgotten. The robots started out learning by rules of logic. They could learn and improve by analyzing vast amounts of data. Were they good or bad?

I don't know. Supposedly they were designed to protect people, to protect humanity."

Kelly laughed, "That sounds like what the Collective wanted to do."

Dan looked over his glasses at Kelly. "True, true."

Walking over to his desk, he said "I thought you might ask this question, so I'm going to read you a memo between two scientists, who must have been friends.

: To Chris D.

I think we have done it. My bot is learning faster than I have seen any of its kind before. It gathers its own data independently. She is learning emotions. We must play it safe. I hear people are destroying them.

: Mark B.

Then the reply

: To Mark B.

I believe my robot is doing as well as yours, even though it is a bit smaller. Our experiment worked. I am fearful for their safety. Let us meet at my house tonight to figure out how to hide them. My place at midnight. God be with us. : Chris D.

Smiling at Kelly. "Now that I have bored you with all these stories the last few days, I thank you for your patience."

Kelly smiled back, "My pleasure! It was enlightening. It's just nice to have a friend to talk to."

Shoop slapped the table. "I agree."

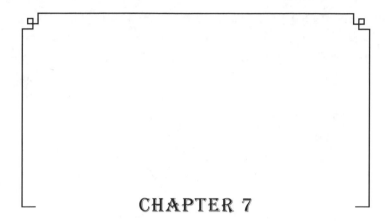

CHAPTER 7

BACK IN THE COLLECTIVE

B art Archer sat in his office on Sunday when all was quiet in the Collective. For three generations his family had overseen the Office of the Silencer. Catching the traitor would have capped off his glorious career. Now there was a stain on not only his name, but also his family's service record. A black mark. He pounded his fist on the desk. How could this happen? He had underestimated those bastards in the outside world. Going back over the events of that day, he acknowledged that he had been distracted by the explosion. It had surprised him. The group that had opposed him on the outside had been small. A handful of country bumpkins is what they were. Their strength had been in the big man. Their leader.

Focus on the future. He told himself. What had he

learned? First, there was a traitor named Billy. Then there was a history teacher writing his book on the history of the world. What could he learn from the book? Could he take over the outside world? Could he use the outside world to take over the Collective? Really, all he wanted was to be the Controller himself. *Was the book the key? What did it have in it?*

Archer leaned back in his chair and smiled. He would have to keep the Controller blind to what he was doing. Easy enough. He would need to go to the town and recruit some outsiders to help him.

If he could not find the book himself then he would just have to take over the town and search it brick by brick. He had already been training a small force of men to fight.

A knock on the door. Archer's Sargent walked in. "Sir! Training went well today, Sir!"

"Sargent Schneider, that's good to hear. Keep me posted. Dismissed."

"Yes sir." The young man turned and left.

Archer scowled. Another Schneider. Cody Schneider was Kim and Kelly's brother. Thinking. *Keep your friends close and keep your enemies closer. Someday I will kill the whole Schneider family. But for now, they may be useful.*

Going down to where the explosion had taken place, he examined the repairs.

A soldier said, "Better than the original, Sir."

"Yes, Yes. Double the lookouts and the guards for the time being."

"Yes Sir."

Archer walked back inside the Collective. The day had not been a waste. He now had a plan. A plan that would make him the Controller of the Collective.

The Controller

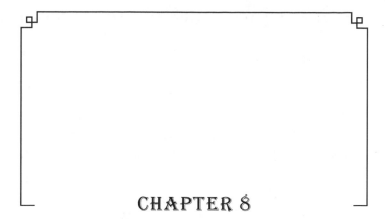

CHAPTER 8

THE CONTROLLER AND THE WOMAN IN BLACK

The Controller of the Collective sat at his desk. A dark-skinned man. Short hair, brown eyes, and a wide nose. One of the hardest working men in the Collective. He straightened his glasses, then stood facing the Woman in Black. What are you calling yourself these days?"

Taking her hood down, she said, "I think names are so trivial. I am your talon that catches whatever prey you send me after. There you have it. Call me Talon."

Smiling at one of his cruelest soldiers, "Fucking marvelous. I have a mission for you."

Talon inquired, "What about the Silencer?"

"He is a damned idiot. You work for me, no one else!"

Seeing that she had irritated him, she stepped back. "Yes sir!"

Another woman entered the office. Smartly dressed, she approached the Controller.

The Controller continued, "I'm just giving Talon her assignment."

The woman nodded as Talon glared at her. Talon had never liked the Controller's advisor.

"Go to the outside world. Take four or five of your best soldiers. Only those that you can trust implicitly. Track down anyone that is writing or telling stories, especially about the Collective."

The advisor Lexa looked at Talon with no emotion on her face. "Your people must not be caught or seen."

"Please!" Talon sneered, "That's a stupid thing to say to a professional."

The Controller took over. "Do this for me and you will be highly rewarded. Learn all you can about the outside world."

Talon saluted, "Spy on them. Eliminate them. Got it. Permission to leave, Sir."

"Dismissed." The Controller turned to Lexa as Talon turned to leave. I want you to keep an eye on the Silencer. After this last bungle I'm not sure what to think of him."

Talon's ears perked up. The Silencer was on the outs. Hmm, remarkably interesting. Her mind changed to her team. First, Manon was the meanest of all the recruits. She was a great leader and fighter. Then there was Alice, Manon's friend. Quick and sneaky smart. She was a bit paranoid at times and liked to be in a position of power. Both girls had no family to make them want to stay in the Collective. Who else? Frank and Jesse were her most loyal people. One more? Frank and Jesse had a friend named Bobby. There it was, a solid five. Bobby was the weakest;

she did not quite trust him. "Oh well! I'll just kill him if he doesn't work out."

The next morning, Talon called the five into her office. "We are going outside on a mission. Prepare to leave in two hours." She stared right at Bobby.

"Oh goody. Do we get to kill anyone?" Alice squealed.

"Maybe." Talon grinned.

Alice hugged Manon, "This will be so fun."

"Dismissed. Be ready in two hours."

All five said in chorus "Yes ma'am."

CHAPTER 9

BILLY AND KELLY LEAVE

Back at Dan Shoop's house Billy had returned. "I don't think anyone followed us, but I don't think we're safe. We need to go into town and buy some supplies." Looking at Kelly, he reminded her "You said you would like to travel across this great country and see that ocean I told you about."

Kelly nodded.

"Here's your chance. I'll draw you some maps."

Dan looked at them both, "Before you leave on this great adventure, I want you to come back here and say goodbye. I have something for both of you."

Billy shook Dan's hand. "Agreed."

About a week later Dan Shoop was dusting some old war medals and admiring his collection. Hard work and research had taken him to some exotic places to find these artifacts.

Staring out the window, his mind shifted to his childhood. As early as he could remember he had been fascinated with history. True history: the stories of men and women, strong and weak who had struggled and forged their mark in the world. There were stories of power and greed mixed in with the love of life and the desire to explore. Taking a book off the shelf titled 'Leadership Secrets by Napoleon', he slowly flipped through the pages. *True history not fake news, he* muttered to himself, looking around. *How could he ever leave all this? All his family was gone. He was the last of his bloodline. These books and medals were his only legacy.*

Musing back through his mind, he remembered a lecture he had given. A strange lecture that he only gave once a year and only to the students whom he deemed ready.

He would begin the lecture by looking out into the hallway as though he was checking for unwanted ears. Shutting the door, he would turn to the class and say, "No notes today, just listen." Then he would add, "tell no one." Sometimes the lecture might be about the beginning of the Collective. Other times it might be about a world long ago. A world with computers and robots. Most of the students thought this all was a fairy tale. There were those few times that Dan was called to the office to face an upset parent that didn't want their child listening to such rubbish.

He recalled the day when he overheard two boys talking in the hallway after such a lecture. The boys were bigger than most and would become good sized men. One boy looked at the other and laughed, "Jake, that whole story was bullshit."

"Now, now, James, you missed the point!" Jake replied.

Looking at James, he said "You see, he wants us to be better than we are now."

"You think too much, Jake. It's all plain bullshit."

Dan put his book back on the shelf and sighed, "Well, at least one may have gotten it." Pulling another book from the shelf, Dan decided to go outside in the sunlight and wait for his friends to return.

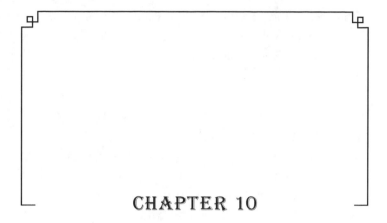

CHAPTER 10

THE GIFT

It had been two weeks since Kelly's torture. Now early April, she was apprehensive about the next stage in her life. Kelly packed her backpack slowly. She was a small girl with short blonde hair, sporting a faded red sweatshirt. She had been through a lot in recent months. Her life had been controlled by others most of the time. Now here was a chance to be on her own and show herself that she was the one in control.

Billy looked over at her. "Are you ready for this?"

Kelly looked at him and smiled slightly. "Ready or not, here I come. I don't think I have a family anymore." Her mind wandered back to her childhood. The joy of being with her family. She recalled how supportive her father had been. He had always put herself and her brother and sister first in his life. Sadly, she thought, *the Collective would have wiped his mind of her existence*. It's just me and what or whomever I find out there in the world. Looking up, she dried her eyes. Kelly patted her dog on the head. Here is my only friend. The dog wagged his tail and looked up at her. "I have named him after my brother," Kelly smiled. "You said you wanted us to see Shoop before we left."

"Yep, one stop and then we go our separate ways. His house is in our general direction."

Off they went, walking through the fields. The dog bounced between them, chasing everything he saw, then running back to join them. After traveling west for an hour and a half, the two climbed a hill which stopped abruptly with a cliff. Billy pointed far in the distance. "That is where you will be traveling." Looking more northward, he pointed. "There is where I'll be going." Indicating the forest below, he said "And there is Dan's house. Let's go say goodbye to our friend." He then led the way to a small opening in the forest. Deep in the trees, a cabin was tucked to one side of a clearing. There, sitting on a rocking chair reading a huge book, sat Dan. Smallish in stature, with short strawberry red hair he squinted at the two as they approached over his small wire framed glasses.

Getting up to greet his friends, he exclaimed "Welcome, welcome!" and hugged them both.

"Can't stay long," said Billy. "We each have a long way to travel."

"Yes, Yes, I know. But I want to give you each something before you go," replied Shoop. "Let's go inside my house." As he opened the door, he looked back, "Too many eyes and ears out here, safer inside."

Billy looked around, "No one followed us, I'm certain."

"Can't be too careful these days," came the reply.

Inside the house was wall after wall of books.

The vastness of knowledge amazed Kelly. "Did you read all these?"

Dan laughed, "Two or three times over. Some I have written." He put his hand on two books on the table. "Here is the true history of the world, not the lies that they want you to believe. Dangerous information if it fell into the wrong hands, inside or outside of the Collective." Shoop went on, "The Collective has been trying to erase any written word they can. The theory is if it wasn't written it didn't happen." Looking at Billy; "Trouble's coming." Pausing, he reached in a small box and pulled two leather beaded necklaces out, handing one to each. There was a thin cylinder pouch at the end as Kelly studied it. The pouch, the size of your finger, was decorated with beads. Looking inside, Kelly found a blue hard-shelled object rather rectangular in shape with a silver tip.

Looking up questioningly, she said "Thank you, it's one of those flash drives you told me about."

Dan nodded, "Yes, and for now let's call it your lucky charm." He continued, "Guard it with your life. The day that your family finds you it just might come in handy."

Kelly puzzled in her mind, *FAMILY? Does Kim, Cody or even her father know she exists?*

Turning to Billy "You my friend should guard yours as well. I am giving you something more important." Picking up a rather large book with a red spine, he looked at Billy. "You told me about the Badlands in the Dakota territory. "What were the words you used?"

Billy replied, "Mako Sicca, land bad, rough terrain and extreme temperatures. But it's my home and my people are there. I've been too long away. My ancestors could not stop the white man from putting them on a reservation, and now I realize I cannot stop the Collective."

Shoop began, "I need you to hide this in those caves you told me about." Billy nodded. Looking at another book on the table, he asked, "What about that one?"

Dan laughed, "No, that's not done yet. It may be more important than the one you're holding."

Kelly interrupted "Who is going to guard that one?"

"Don't know yet. I hope I find someone just like you, my friend. I mentioned a grass roots movement against the Collective. This book is a way to educate the people out here about the Collective. To educate them about the truth is my goal."

Billy and Kelly walked to the door. Billy turned back "You going to be ok?" Dan shrugged. "Not sure about that. My gut tells me I may not make it out of this. My only hope is that these books do." He continued "Don't worry, I've had a good life."

Billy smiled, "I think you need a friend, now that I will be gone. Look up a new man in town. His name is Sid Finch. He has taken over the newspaper in Muddville."

Dan nodded, "Thanks, I'll do that."

Kelly and Billy left that day wondering about the mystery that Dan had laid before them. They set up camp that night and enjoyed their last meal together. It was a bright sunny morning as they woke up. Walking a little distance in silence, Kelly knew that their paths would split soon. When the time came, Billy stopped. "Here it is, Kid. I'm going North and you need to angle Northwest." Kelly's face paled. "You'll be ok, I know you and your ability." Kelly took a deep breath. She wished her brother and sister were here with her. The bold first step began her new adventure.

Was Kim and Cody's life this hard?

CHAPTER 11

JAKE ALLEN

One year earlier.

It was a quiet afternoon in Muddville. Jake Allen was packing up his room. He paused to look around his old classroom and listened to the sounds of the town outside.

A knock on the door. The door opened and a barrel-chested man stuck his head in. "Well, well I hear you're going to the dark side."

Jake laughed, facing his friend grinning. Yep, the School Board made it official last night. I am the new Superintendent of Schools. It means more money."

Wes closed the gap between the two and shook Jake's hand. "You know it's supposed to be about the kids, not the money, right?"

"Now Wes." Jake stated, "I can help teachers be better teachers."

Wes laughed, "You're a dreamer. All you will end up

doing is putting out fires every day. Eventually you'll end up pissing off the teachers you wanted to help."

Jake got serious, "No, I won't."

Wes turned to leave. Stopping at the door. "All I have to say is that you were one of the best teachers we've ever had here. Good luck to you."

Jake finished packing and carried his large box of books out of the room, shutting the door for the last time. A feeling of excitement and sadness washed over him at the same time. He left the High School and headed across the street to the Superintendent's office. He was enjoying the sunny day and he took a deep breath of fresh air.

A new beginning: he stepped into the Superintendent's office. Instantly Jake was greeted by a big smile. "Welcome Mr. Allen. Let me show you to your office" said the secretary.

Jake smiled back, "Thank you Karen."

Walking back to his new office, he thought it had only been a couple of years since Karen had been a student in his classroom. She had earned a B in his class. Not that she was not smart, she was simply happy with a B.

"Here we go, Sir." Karen turned to leave. "Call me if you need anything."

"Sure thing" Jake said, peering into his new office. *Where do I start first*, he wondered?

That night at dinner Jake and his wife talked about his new job. "I want to do a good job. I want to make Muddville Schools better."

His wife grabbed his hand and squeezed it, "You'll do fine, Honey."

Jake frowned, "The School Board expects a lot. I have

to find a way to improve the schools and have data to prove it." Scratching his head, "I wonder how I can do it?"

That night he lay in bed for a long time, thinking about his new job and his new problems.

CHAPTER 12

SID FINCH

At the very moment that Jake Allen was walking his books over to the Superintendent's office, Carl Brown sat in Pat's Tavern eating a BLT. It was a much-needed lunch break. Just down the street was his newspaper office. He was the reporter, the writer, the editor, and the printer all in one. He was the Muddville Times and he was very tired. Sipping his cold beer, he thought some people in the town would not approve of beer during the workday. He was ninety-two, who cares what they think.

The door to the tavern opened and in walked a man. Looking around the bar, he removed his sunglasses and sat down two stools away from Carl.

Carl's reporters eye looked the man over. The man was dusty and a little sweaty. He must have been walking a long way. A stranger… he must be new in town. Long hair in a ponytail, sunglasses, and a long mustache; quite a character.

The bartender walked over. "Howdy, what'll ya have?"

"The coldest beer you got." came the reply.

Carl Brown moved next to the man. Maybe this man could help him, or if nothing else this could be a story for the paper. "Name's Carl Brown and who might you be?"

The man grinned, "Me, I am Sid Finch, the last of the great story tellers."

Carl chuckled, "I run the newspaper here in town."

Sid continued grinning and his eyes sparkled with amusement. "I just got into town. I'm from down south. I've been a wrestler, an artist, and a teacher. I've been traveling the world. There you have it; my short story. I kind of have in mind finding a place to call home for a while."

Carl laughed and took a long drink of his beer. "Well now I have a proposal for you. What say you come work for me? I'll show you the ropes at the paper. I'll check you out to see if you can handle it. You check the town out to see if it suits you. If all works out, you can buy me out. You find a home and I get to retire, getting a much-needed rest. Reporting is quite easy. You just report on things that happen in town. You are a storyteller. That's what you would be doing. My greatest desire is that the Muddville Times keeps running."

Sid liked the idea and the two shook hands.

Another new beginning.

HUNTING SEASON

Talon

CHAPTER 13

TALON EXPLORES

Talon's group moved forward in the outside world at the same time as Billy and Kelly were preparing for their journey. She wore a black uniform and had her knives strapped to her side. She also wore a black hooded cape that covered most of her face. Starting at a brisk pace, she led her band of people away from the Collective. Manon and Alice were quick to follow. Jesse and Frank came next with Bobby straggling behind. Keeping to secluded and woody places, they made it to a point that Talon deemed safe for them. They pitched their camp, which would be home for some time. Talon watched her people intently, overseeing every move they made. Manon seemed at home instantly. Jesse and Frank talked about things they might see in the outside world. Were there fortunes to be made? Alice seemed to be a loner although she did talk to Manon occasionally.

Bobby preferred to stay to himself. He seemed a bit nervous and edgy. *Would he be trouble?*

The next morning Talon woke everyone up early. Drawing a clock in the dirt she pointed out. "We are six. I will head out towards one o'clock. Manon at three. Alice at five. Jesse is seven and Frank is nine. Bobby you are eleven. Got it? Walk in the direction I told you to until the sun is at its highest point. Make a mental note of all that you see. Then come back here and we will make a map of the information that you have gathered. Yes?"

"Yes Ma'am."

Each headed off.

Talon moved out through the woods. The few houses were mostly vacant. Her route seemed flat. At noon she turned and headed back to camp. *Could she trust her people to be as observant as herself?* She sat waiting for her group to return. Bobby was the first, running into camp out of breath. Manon was next then came Frank and Jesse. Alice slowly walked in last. Giving them time to rest, Talon used her time to draw a map and note what she had seen. The rest of their observations would help her complete the map and then she would be able to decide where to strike first.

That night over dinner Talon announced, "Story time."

She began describing what she saw. What she deemed important. The number of people she saw. Important landmarks that caught her eye. She finished her observations and looked up. "Now it's your turn. Manon you're up."

Manon began, "Mostly flat country. Some vacant houses like you saw, but I reckon that if you walked a full day you would see many big buildings. A city, I think. I don't know if people live there."

"Good, good." Talon smiled at Manon. "Alice?"

"Sorry Ma'am. I spent the entire day in woods and weeds. I saw nothing really."

Talon nodded, "That's okay, that's information we need. Jesse?"

He was beaming, "I found Muddville. Isn't that where the farmers that attacked us were from?"

"Good." Talon acknowledged. "Don't get too excited, we have other fish to fry before we look at Muddville itself. Frank?"

"Mostly like you saw Ma'am. The farther west I went the less houses and fewer people I saw."

See this is what we need to know. To the east there are more people and to the west farms and less people." Talon snapped, "What in the hell is that thing you're playing with Bobby?"

Bobby held up a gold watch. "I found it."

"Found! You're a liar. What did you do?"

Bobby sputtered, "Well, I found a man sleeping under a tree, so I just took it. He woke up and chased me. I lost him. He never saw my face, I swear it."

Talon walked over to Bobby and hit him with the back of her hand. The blow was so powerful that he was knocked some distance from where he had been sitting. Crumpled he cowered. "Sorry."

Frank began laughing at Bobby. Talon picked up the watch and tossed it over to Jesse. "Nice work today. From now on we take nothing unless I approve it. Got it?"

In unison, the group said, "Got it."

CHAPTER 14

THE SILENCER
FINDS HELP

B art Archer stepped outside of the Collective. Unlike Talon, he was alone. Having held training sessions outside with some of his men, he felt quite comfortable out here. This was a world he could conquer. He wanted no one to hold him back and no one to know what he was doing. Quietly and slowly he moved around the area watching people from afar. After three days of hunting he found Muddville. He spent the next day moving around the outskirts of the town. Flat to the north, hilly to the south. Traveling to the east of town, he entered a deep woods. He moved slowly through the shadows. Several hours later he came upon a small cabin. Two young men were splitting wood. A boy was playing with a dog nearby. Stepping out of the shadows, the dog began to bark as Archer approached the cabin.

The work stopped. The skinnier of the two young men yelled, "Howdy Mister."

Archer greeted them with a smile. "It's been a long walk. Could you boys give me a drink?"

The boys looked at each other, "Sure come on in and sit a spell." Tod, the skinnier of the two, offered Archer a chair. Jay, the more physical looking of the young men sat a glass of water down on the table.

Archer took a long drink of the water. Looking up, he made up a name. "I'm Ben and who are you boys?"

The skinnier one began to speak, "I'm Tod and this here is my brother Jay and that there's the baby of the family; Koz."

Archer looked at the youngest of the Keys. He looked rather big for his age. The boy's hair was a mess. "Why's his name Koz?"

Jay laughed, looking at the younger Keys boy, "Hey, why'd ya set that cat on fire the other day?"

The boy, disgusted with his older brothers, turned to leave. "Koz I wanted to."

The brothers began to laugh so hard they could barely remain in their seats.

Finally, between laughs Tod said, "That's the answer he gives to everything. That's what we started calling him and the name stuck, 'Koz'."

Archer got serious, "I have some money that I'm willing to give you boys. All you must do is tell me about Muddville. When you give me information I can use, I will give you money."

Tod and Jay looked at each other. "Deal. What do you want to know?"

"Let's start with the history teacher in town and his book." Archer said, quietly putting money on the table.

Tod laughed, "Bastard, Shoop's class was the most boring class I ever had."

"Tell me where the book is, and I will give you this money. Get that book for me and I'll double it." Getting up and standing in the doorway, he looked back as the boys looked at his silhouette. "You tell anyone what we talked about and I will kill you all." Archer vanished, leaving the Keys brothers staring.

CHAPTER 15

THE KILLING

Talon took her time scouting the surrounding woods and fields in all directions around Muddville. They watched travelers on the road. Listening to conversations, gossip and news as people talked to one another. Silently, Talon moved about the countryside and began to pick targets. A few people were found dead in the morning by family members. Others had their houses burned. Talon had her people bury or burn most of the evidence of their existence. To the locals it became a very fearful time. No real clues existed for family members to convince the Sheriff to investigate further.

Old and young became targets, especially if they told a story, sang a song, or even painted a picture. People began disappearing without a trace as though they had never existed.

One afternoon, Manon and Alice hid behind some trees

watching a small group that had gathered. A man stood on a platform in front of the people that had gathered there.

Men, women, and children applauded as he introduced himself. "I am a storyteller! If you enjoy what you are about to hear my wife has a hat." He pointed to her. "If you think my story is really good pay me what you think it's worth. If you hate my story pay me nothing." He then began to weave a wonderful yarn as the crowd became enthralled.

Manon looked over at Alice, "Let's go tell Talon." Slowly they backed away from the gathering. Talon was delighted, "Good work! Manon, go back and follow the storyteller and see where they set up camp. Then come back and get the rest of us."

Manon sprinted off.

The family sat having dinner around a campfire. It was still light outside, although the sun was setting. Manon saw them settle in. Their camp was in the middle of a deep woods. Talon would think this was a perfect place for an ambush. Manon silently went back and found Talon.

Back at the campfire, a boy was begging his father. "Come on Dad tell me your new story."

"Well it's not quite finished, Son."

"Ah! Come on Dad, please…. I know it'll be good. You're one of the best storytellers around."

"Now Brucie, you need to finish your dinner and do the dishes before any storytelling!" his Grandmother commanded. She was the one who had started calling him Brucie when he was young. Now that's what everyone called him.

Brucie hung his head "Okay Grandma, when I'm done with all that, you'll tell me it's bedtime. I just turned thirteen. I should be old enough to stay up a little later."

His father laughed, "I'll tell the story tonight. Finish your meal."

Grandma chuckled, "You're just a baby."

"Am not," Brucie glared at the old woman.

Things were being cleaned up. "Almost done here, Dad"

"Okay, go clean up in the stream below. Get some of the day's dirt off that big boy's body," his Dad laughed.

"Okay Dad." Brucie wandered off, following a small path down to the stream. Taking off his pants and shirt he waded into the stream. The water was cold, and it took his breath away. Splashing some water on himself he tried to clean up the best he could. Grandma would check, he just knew it. Putting his clothes back on, he stood there for a few minutes watching the water swirl.

At that very moment Talon struck. Jesse stepped up behind the wife as Talon stepped up behind the grandmother. Knives to throats; they never had a chance. Living one second, dead the next. The storyteller turned and screamed as Frank tackled him, knifing the man in the chest several times. Then silence as they all looked around.

Brucie began to walk up towards the firelight. It was dark now. As he moved forward, a pair of strange silhouettes danced past the firelight. Brucie froze. A few moments passed as he puzzled at what he saw. He took a step and then another.

A shriek rang out.

Brucie froze again. Then dropping down on his belly, he lay quietly. *What was going on*? Slowly, ever so slowly he crawled forward. Then another cry. It was his Dad's voice; he was sure of it. Then silence. The next sounds were like things being drug around the campfire. Brucie quietly crawled forward. A little distance from the camp he found three fallen trees stacked on top of each other. He lay behind them; he could just make out the campsite.

A figure with a black hood sat on the edge of the camp, "Burn it all."

"All of it?" A man questioned.

"Everything, you fool." The voice sounded like a woman to Brucie's ears. He lay motionless, afraid to take a breath. The man by the fire picked up something.

Pleading "Just one little trinket?"

In a flash, the woman was across the camp, her hand on the man's throat. The man gasped for air, but the hand on his throat allowed none. "Please." But that came out as a rasp. The woman lifted the man up. His eyes bulged. Her fingers dug in deep around his throat. With a quick twist of her wrist she ripped out everything in her hand. Blood squirted and the man collapsed in a pile. Turning to the other four, saying as calm as could be "Burn everything, please." She went back to her seat silently watching.

The four nodded. They too, were dressed in black. The first man was medium sized and had blonde, shaggy hair. The second man had a stout frame. There were two other women: one with long, brown hair and the other with short, black hair. The short haired girl seemed to be enjoying the whole thing. The whole group looked evil to the young boy. Brucie shivered as he looked at the sinister characters. The one with the hood giving orders scared him the most. She seemed to be the boss.

Once, during the night, as the fire began to burn down, the lady turned and stared right at Brucie. Or at least that is what he thought.

He laid stiff and silent as he watched his family burn.

The fire was now a matter of coals. The Lady stood up, straightening her cloak. "Move out." The group silently followed her out of camp. Just before they went out of sight Brucie swore she turned and looked back at him. Then swirled and was gone.

Brucie remained hidden, in shock that whole night and then through that next day and night. During the night it began to rain. Daring not to move, he lay soaking wet and cold. Finally getting up the courage, he slowly rose. He checked over the camp. Nothing. Ashes. No trace of Mom, Dad, or even Grandma.

Manon and the group followed Talon back to their camp. No one talked. No one said a word about Talon killing Bobby. In Manon's mind he deserved it.

Brucie remembered his father telling him that water would always lead him to people. Towns were always built near water. Following the stream as it became bigger, his hopes rose. He could find someone to help him. Anyone that could save him. Time passed and he became hungry. His feet ached as he walked along the bank, tree branches and bushes tearing at his arms and legs. Tears rolled. Alone, he trudged for a day and a half with no hope in sight.

"Now what do I do?"

Brucie

CHAPTER 16

BRUCIE FINDS MUDDVILLE

Cold and tired, Brucie shuffled into Muddville that April day. Desperate to find food, he began to poke around into different shops. But the owners had no interest in helping a dirty little kid. One shopkeeper yelled, "Get out! We don't need filth like you around here!" He was demoralized. Looking at his reflection in a store window. He admitted it to himself. He was a dirty mess.

Cutting through a back alleyway, he was trying to avoid all the people that were out that day. He moved down the alley not really knowing where to go. Then WHAM, he was on his face and this big ugly boy was staring down at him.

"Well, well, what do we have here?" As the boys behind him began to circle Brucie, laughing, one of them said "Hey Koz, looks like a reject to me." Another round of laughter.

Brucie wiped blood from his nose, looking up at the bully. Koz started kicking him with his foot.

"We dub you Sir Reject. And, Oh, by the way, you don't belong in Muddville. I'm feeling nice today, so I'll give you five seconds before I beat the crap out of you."

"Five seconds is all I need!" Brucie laughed. Quick like a shot he was gone.

Now Koz was the joke. Laughter erupted. "You didn't see that kid as being fast, did you?" The bully's face turned bright red with rage. Punching the fence behind him, Koz screamed, "I'm gonna get you."

Brucie's life changed; he became a thief. Living on the edge of town, he developed a routine. Getting to know when the restaurants put old food in the trash. When the bakers baked. All kinds of things. Sure, there was still some run ins with Koz and the gang. They were always setting up traps and ambushes. He got smarter and faster. It all became a game. Traveling about town when people are not around much. He did get into some fights and took a few lumps. Besides Koz, there was Sheriff James he had to avoid. All in all, he became a bandit king.

A month after Brucie arrived in town he dared something risky. He had it all planned out in his mind. Watch the baker. Then when he turned his back, run in, grab a loaf of bread and sprint out. Easy peasy.

He stood watching the baker. The baker finally turned to go check his ovens. Brucie was off like a shot. Inside, he grabbed the first bundle of bread he saw. Turning, he ran.

WHAM! Again, he was on his face and guess who was laughing? Koz. The store owner came out screaming at him. Turning to run, a nearby man picked Brucie up by the collar. "Now hold on boy." The baker was still yelling, "He stole my bread! Call the Sheriff!"

Still holding on to Brucie, the man reached in his pocket. Pulling out some money, he handed it to the baker. "Look give the kid a break. He looks hungry. I'll take care of him, just let it go. Forget the whole thing happened."

The baker seemed to be calming down, seeing that the man had given him more money than the bread was worth. "Ok, only if I never see that boy in my shop again. If I see him there once, I will call the Sheriff on him and you, Sid Finch."

"Deal." Said Sid.

Koz wasn't happy with the results of the morning. "Mister, you can't do that, he's trouble."

Sid looked at Koz, "Maybe he is, maybe he's not. That's up to me and him to decide, not you. Now git."

Walking Brucie back to his newspaper office. "What's your name?"

"Brucie." He wasn't too sure what to think of the strange looking man with long hair.

Sid continued, "I'll offer you a good meal tonight and a place to sleep. Tomorrow morning, I will show you what I do and what I need done. If it suits you, then you work for me and I give you free room and board."

"If I don't like it?" Brucie asked.

Sid smiled, "Then you're free to go."

The next morning Brucie was shown around. It seemed easy to him. He would be fed and no more sleeping in the cold. Was there a downside? He couldn't think of any. "Okay, I'd like to stay with you Mister Finch."

"Excellent." The man clapped his hands together. "We will make a good team. Oh, just call me Sid."

Days later, as Brucie and Sid became friends, Brucie told Sid about the killing of his parents. "Dad was a storyteller, much like you." Sid patted the boy on his back. "Well, your story has yet to be written, and right now you're in a good place."

CHAPTER 17

SID MEETS SHOOP

Dan Shoop walked into the Muddville Times newspaper office. Looking around, he spotted a long-haired man. Bushy long mustache. Walking over, he introduced himself. "I am Dan Shoop, the history teacher at the High School." The man turned around and smiled. A boy continued working on the printing press.

"Ah, yes, I have heard about you."

"All good I hope?" replied Dan.

"Yes." came the answer. "Quite good." Shaking Dan's hand, "I am Sid Finch, the new owner of the Muddville Times. I have just taken over after Mr. Brown's ownership of forty-two years."

Dan continued, "A friend of mine told me to seek you out. Said we might have mutual interests. His name is Billy."

"Hmm. An Indian fellow, I believe. Some of the people in town have mentioned him." Sid replied.

"Yes"

Dan turned abruptly around. "Gotta get back to my classroom. Could you meet me at Pat's tonight?"

Sid smiled, "Sure."

"See you then!" Dan swiftly left, leaving Sid puzzled.

Pat's Tavern was the meeting place for most of the locals. A small store front with a big green sign in white letters spelling out PAT'S. One could walk in and walk down a long hallway to the back door. A bar was on the left-hand side and three tables stood on the right. A door opened after the tables. The opening allowed access to a larger back room with more tables. Poorly lit and rarely cleaned, the bar was home to those that loved a good beer. Who was Pat? No one knew or they had plain forgotten. The name would last for eternity.

That night at Pat's Tavern Sid walked in. He was confronted by the smell of stale beer and tobacco smoke. He looked around and spied the little man he had just met. Walking over to Dan, he sat down. "So, what's the big deal?" Continuing, "I've heard some good stories about you. You're a hard teacher, expecting the best from every student. Yet, your love for history is unsurpassed."

"Well, you know a little about me, but what about you? What's your story?"

Sid laughed, "Well, I come from a small-town upbringing. I was an athlete in school, a wrestler. A good one, I think, but then again, your history wipes that all away. Tried my hand at teaching but found that mediocre people don't want to be great. Travelled the world to some extent. I was a risk taker at times. Now I've taken the newspaper over from a ninety-year-old man. And just maybe, if I play my cards right, I'll find a home."

Dan snickered, "If the Muddville people accept you. How'd you get the newspaper?"

Sid recalled, "I had just gotten into town a year ago. Not knowing what to do I stopped here for some lunch. Sitting at the bar, I'm next to an old man named Carl Brown. We got to talking and found we had mutual interests in watching people and telling stories. He says he's tired and wants to retire. Then, out of nowhere he offers me the newspaper. Says I can start working for him and learn about what he does. End of the story, I buy him out. He told me it wasn't too hard writing local stories about rescuing a cat out of a tree or reporting about the Keys brothers getting in a fight. I should just watch the town and tell their stories."

Shoop began to laugh, "Those Keys boys gave me a lot of trouble in class."

"So, there's my story. Why would that Indian friend of yours want us to get together?"

Shoop answered, "Probably because he thought I needed a friend or an ally."

Sid protested "Ally? I don't even know you."

Dan looked around "Well, I trust Billy and so I am going to trust you. Do you know anything about the Collective?"

"Some." said Sid. "I've heard the stories."

Dan leaned closer. "Not stories, they are real. And Billy's been there." Dan shared Billy's story and then Kelly's story. "Now they have both left Muddville. Just in time I'd say." Looking Sid in the eyes, he said, "Bad things are coming, I'm telling you. Awfully bad things."

Sid looked back "Yes. I have heard those tales. Most recently I have taken in a homeless boy. He's been telling me about his parents being killed by a woman in black."

Dan gasped; his body began to tremble. "They are closer than I thought. This means that any writer or storyteller is in grave danger." Emphatically, he finished, "The Collective is out hunting. Your newspaper is a threat. All my history books are a threat. They will be ruthless in reaching their goal."

Standing up quickly, Shoop said, "I'm sorry, I've got to go. Plans must be made. I would advise you to do the same. See you later, my new friend." Shoop threw some money on the table. Swiftly he left.

Sid sat puzzled by all he had heard. *What should he make of it?* Walking back home, thoughts of danger kept ringing in his mind. Peering over his shoulder every now and then, he made it back home.

Telling Brucie of his meeting with Shoop, he said "Listening to his stories and the death of your parents, I'm concerned. This would be a great story. I should investigate the murders for the newspaper. You keep an eye out for those people that killed your parents."

Brucie nodded and a chill ran down his spine. *Was he even safe with Sid?*

Koz

CHAPTER 18

THE KEYS BROTHERS

One evening the Keys brothers sat eating dinner. They had worked hard that day. Tod looked at Jay, "It's too bad that Mom and Dad ain't here to help us out."

Jay sadly smiled, "Yeah, they were always good to us. It was that damned Wetzel clan that kilt them."

Tod finished chewing his bite of food. "Now Jay, you know damn well it was Dad who killed one of their family first. We're just lucky they ain't coming after us."

Jay sighed, "But we need money, Tod."

The boys sat in silence. Koz, although listening, had never stopped eating.

Jay began again, "We got cousins down in the valley by the river. We could go live with them."

Tod hammered the table, "No! This place is ours and we're not giving it up."

At that very moment, there was a knock at the door. Tod

got up to answer it. Before he reached the door, Bart Archer stepped in. "You boys made me dinner! You didn't have to do that." Pulling a chair over to the table he sat down.

Tod stared at the man. "Didn't think we'd see you again."

"Well, I couldn't break up a good team, could I? Got anything to tell me?"

Koz was the first to speak, "That new girl in town and that redskin Billy left and headed out west. I heard that Billy was headed to the Dakotas. Wherever that is."

Tod blurted out, "How the hell did you hear that?"

Koz beamed, "Some of the guys in my gang told me."

Archer chuckled. Tossing a gold coin over to Koz. "Well done, kid." He already knew about the two leaving town and was wondering if it would be worth chasing that Billy fellow.

Seeing the money Koz got, Jay began to speak. That history teacher you asked about - I know that he had two books he was writing. At least that is what he had when I was in his class."

Tod jumped in, eager to earn some money himself. "Remember that one day lecture he always gave." Pausing he looked around. All eyes were on him. "Crazy Shoop didn't let us take notes that day. Shoop talked about inventions called computers and technology and something called AI. It all seemed like bullshit to most of us." Looking at Archer, "Is there something to it?"

Archer stayed calm. *No need to let the boys know anything.* "Might be something, and then again it might be nothing." Wondering, *could this technology be the key he needed to take out the Controller?*" Stacking a small bag of coins on the table. "Good job. Keep this up and I'll give you more. Find those books and you boys will be rich men. Standing up, he left without shutting the door behind him, letting in the cool night air.

The three brothers sat in silence with visions of riches in their minds.

Lexa

CHAPTER 19

SECRETS TOLD

B ack in the Collective, a purple haired woman walked to her job at the Controller's headquarters. As she came to a street corner, a man stopped her. They moved off to one side, out of the way of most of the people. They each looked around to make certain no one was listening.

The man lowered his voice saying, "They're both out."

Lexa nodded; "I knew Talon had been sent out. What is the Silencer doing?" The man leaned in close. "The word is, he's planning on attacking some town out there called Muddville."

"What!" She gasped too loudly. Looking around to make sure she had not drawn anyone's attention. "You've done well. Keep your eyes open."

The man nodded, "I am your servant."

Lexa smiled her funny little smile. "I'll take care of our problem. Oh! By the way, can you keep track of the

Schneiders for me? Especially Kim and Cody. I want to know every move they make."

"Yes Ma'am" came the reply as the man left.

Lexa continued walking down the street and turned into the Collective's main office building.

Moments later, there was a knock at the Controller's door.

"Enter." came the command.

Lexa entered the Controller's office.

The Controller looked up, "Ah, it's you, Lexa. What do you want?"

"Sir, I have information for you."

Leaning back in his chair, the Controller asked, "What is it?"

Approaching the desk, Lexa spoke smoothly, "I have just learned that the Silencer has been working behind your back. He has organized a unit of approximately 200 security forces and armed them. Furthermore, he plans to attack a town outside of the Collective."

The Controller stood up. "Where and when will this happen?"

"It will be at a town called Muddville. The attack will happen soon."

Beginning to pace, he said, "I do not like him going behind my back. He is too ambitious for his own good. The real problem is the town gets destroyed and then the outsiders would retaliate against us in a big way. The backlash would be terrible." Stopping, deep in thought, he said "How would we stop this?"

Lexa began, "You're saying if the Silencer succeeds, Muddville people will die. This will awaken more of the outside world to our presence. The retaliation could be quite damaging to the Collective."

The Controller nodded his head.

Lexa continued, "You have two options. One, you hire Talon to kill him. Two, we tell the Muddville people and they kill the Silencer. You are right about the backlash, Sir."

The Controller went back to his desk. "Our way of life must be maintained at any cost. The Collective belief and mindset have been maintained for decades. I will not lose that on my watch." Staring at Lexa, "Can you tell the Muddville people about the Silencer's attack? We may lose a few of the security forces, but that is better than thousands of the Collective. Then, work hard to cover up the knowledge of the Collective." The Controller rubbed his chin, "You see, sacrifice the few to save the many. Can you make all this happen?"

Lexa straightened, "Yes sir. It needs to be done now."

Shouting, "What are you waiting for? GO now! GO!"

CHAPTER 20

THE WARNING

Lexa left the Collective without anyone noticing her absence. She walked in to Muddville. A quaint little town. Lexa had not anticipated how backward and conservative the town would be. She was overdressed and stuck out among these simpletons. Heads turned as she explored the town. Greetings were exchanged. A bit more formal than locals were used to. Lexa stopped to talk to an old woman tending her flowers, then waved goodbye and headed to the Superintendent's Office.

The Superintendent's Office sat on the north side of town. It was a tan colored building across the street from the High School and Middle School.

Lexa walked into the entrance, smartly dressed. She had short purple hair brushed all to the right side. The secretary sat behind a counter. Looking up, she said, "May I help you Ma'am?"

The lady smiled back, "May I see Mr. Allen, please?" Karen, the secretary stood up. "Are you a parent?" The lady shook her head, "Absolutely not. I have important information for his ears only." Karen frowned, feeling put off by the lady's arrogance. "Please wait here while I tell Mr. Allen that you are here."

The secretary opened the door. "Sir, are you busy?" Jake sighed. "Not another parent?"

"No Sir, I don't think that's it." A lady; says it's important".

"Okay let her in."

Walking in, the beautiful lady stood in front of Jake Allen's desk. She was as tall as Jake himself. Jake rose and shook her hand, noticing her stunning haircut. "What can I do for you, Miss?"

She decided to be direct and to the point. "Mr. Allen, I have some information for you. You are the person in charge of Muddville, correct?" *Make him feel important.*

"So to speak." Jake answered.

"There will be an attack on your town in a couple of days. They will come from the south with a force of approximately 200. You should have time enough to prepare for them. That's all I know, but the information is credible, and you should take this seriously." She turned sharply and began to leave.

"Wait," Jake said a bit stunned. "What's your name?"

The lady had turned quickly and was halfway down the hall. Yelling over her shoulder. "That's unimportant."

Jake rubbed the top of his head "Wow!?"

Yelling out the door, "Karen, get Sheriff James to come over please."

"Now?" Came the voice from the other room.

"Well, as soon as possible. Thank you."

Now What?

The Silencer

CHAPTER 21

THE CRIME

The count was never really recorded. Some say the Silencer's force was one hundred. There were others that have said it was closer to two hundred soldiers.

The Silencer was a tall man with dark brown hair and eyes. His eyebrows sat on top of his eyes, giving him a look of a constant frown. He enjoyed dressing in his crisp, clean black uniform. He had been in the service of the Controller all his life with a nearly spotless record. Just one blemish, which irritated him immensely. Now he had a chance to shine and show one and all his power.

He was going to go outside of the Collective and teach those bastards a lesson. These were the people that had helped his prisoner escape. The only mistake in a long service. This idea, his plan had been schemed up long ago. Slowly over the months he had sent men out to beg, borrow, or steal weapons from the farmers on the outside.

Men in twos or threes acquiring small amounts of guns at random times of the year were never noticed. The Silencer trained these men, loosely called soldiers. All they had to do in the past was guard and maintain the Collective. The tricky part was the marksmanship training. Although they did train hard, shooting at targets does not simulate a live battle scene. This was to be a fight. A major victory for the Collective and promote him in the eyes of the Controller. As plans were executed, it was necessary for the troops to position themselves. Meetings were held with squad leaders, maps were drawn, and assignments given. Now that he knew that the books were in or around Muddville, it made this attack a logical choice.

Cody was in on all the meetings, having gained favor with the Silencer. "Are you ready for this?"

Cody saluted "Yes, Commander. Permission to speak freely, Sir."

The Silencer's eyes met the young man's eyes, "Granted."

"It seems to me that you have not given us time to scout the area."

Brushing Cody off, "No need, we will recon as we go. This is a surprise attack and whatever group of townsfolk face us will be pathetic." Cody saluted the Commander again and turned and left the office.

Cody muttered to his friend Thompson as they walked down the hallway. "This is crazy." Thompson felt the same way but said nothing.

He stopped by his sister's office. "Hey Kim, let's have dinner tonight. Come over to my place."

"Okay, sounds great."

Later that evening, Kim arrived at Cody's apartment.

Their small talk began with all the niceties, but as the night was concluding Kim could see Cody appeared edgy. "What's wrong?" she asked.

"It's nuts, I tell you; he's taking us out to get into a fight. He's calling it a battle. Kim! We have never even been in a battle. He wants to grab some glory for himself."

Kim looked puzzled, "I haven't heard a word about this."

"That's because he's doing it on his own and hasn't told the Controller. Get this, I was waiting to see him today to discuss the fight and I overheard him and the Lady in Black talking."

"What was that about?" Kim questioned.

Cody continued, "She asked him what he was up to and he said it was none of her business. They started yelling. The Silencer said he was the most powerful man in the Collective and that everyone feared him. He continued by reminding her that he had trained her himself. She demanded in on what he was planning. His response was NO. Adding that she never planned things on her own but just used other people's plans for her own benefit. Finishing, he said 'You are my subordinate, dismissed.' She stomped out, slamming the door. Sis, I had to work hard not to laugh."

Kim shook her head. "Best stay out of their way."

When dinner was finished the two hugged, and Kim looked at Cody. "Be careful."

He looked at her saying, "I'll try Sis. I believe in the Collective. This scares me."

The day arrived, and the Silencer's forces moved out through rough terrain. Cody was scouting that day and saw signs of some Muddville men. They were just south of the town. Throughout his three years in the Silencer's service, he was one of the most experienced of all the troops.

His search for signs of an enemy had not been a pleasant one. Crawling through dense and shadowy woods had reinforced his belief that this had been poorly planned. It had been raining as he scouted. He made it back to the Silencer just as the rain stopped. The Silencer was in a highly agitated state, almost appearing gleeful.

The Silencer gave the command to move forward. The men had been placed into three squads. Cody's friend Thompson led group one. Reynolds had group two and Cody led group three. Thompson was ordered forward to where Cody had seen the enemy. It was tough going in the soggy woods. Several of the men became helplessly lost, detached from the main unit. Those lost started yelling for help from their comrades.

Back in Muddville, Sheriff James had rounded up many willing volunteers. The Muddville Pride turned out many hunters and farmers. People that were used to handling a gun. Sid volunteered. What good newspaper man wouldn't want to be in the middle of the story? James had gathered this group on the highest ground in the area, looking for any signs of would be attackers. And sure enough, down below in the dense forest could be heard yelling. "There's your sign. You people get low and take aim. Wait till I tell you to shoot."

The ambush was set, now just the waiting.

Cody looked at the Silencer "We're still attacking?"

"Absolutely!" came the reply. As the Silencer's men slowly formed and advanced, they found themselves in a deep ravine. The Sheriff had sent two men to check out the yelling and spot the enemy. Sure enough, they saw Thompson's troopers. Turning and running back to the Sheriff, one scout yelled back, "Oh no! You got us licked now." Laughing as they thought about their trick on the attackers.

That made the Silencer's men excited and they rushed forward in disorder. Thompson leading the way. This could be a chance for glory and a promotion. Cody watched the first group. The thought running through his head was *They're moving too fast. They're out of control.*

As Thompson's men reached some fifty yards from the top of the ravine, they heard a sound of ringing and the rattle of guns. Next came the hissing of bullets and the forest was filled with smoke. A deafening roar; a mix of cheering from the Muddville side and terrified yells from the troops down in the ravine. Sheets of metal missiles ripped through the troops. There was nowhere to hide. Advancing was the only option, which was easy pickings for the Muddville militia. This was a slaughter, plain and simple. So unexpected and so precise was the shooting that the Silencer's men died where they stood. The few living pressed forward, continuing into the ambush, and losing their lives. Thompson was the first to take a bullet to his head and one to the chest.

The Silencer looked on grimly. Turning to Reynolds, he said "Go around to their right and flank them! Cody, hold your ground until he begins his attack. Go now!" Both men saluted and returned to their units.

There was a pause in the shooting. A few of the first group lay wounded, still trying to shoot at their enemy. But the snipers on the ridge were picking them off one by one.

Reynolds' men moved through the underbrush trying to find the right place to attack.

At that very moment Sheriff James turned to Dan Shoop. "What would you do if you were them?"

Shoop scanned the terrain. "There…" Pointing to a space on his left. "I'd try to sneak in around us."

The Sheriff bellowed, pointing at a group of men, "You there, follow Shoop and do what he says."

Shoop took off running with about a third of the Sheriff's men. They found a good spot and dug in.

Reynolds had reached a spot where he felt like he should attack. This was the closest that the Silencer's men had been to the enemy all day. Normally a brave man, Reynolds hesitated. The screams of the dying men in the first charge had unnerved him. That hesitation allowed Shoop's men time to secure their position.

Reynolds stood and charged. Shoop's men stood their ground with a devastating volley. Reynolds had taken three steps when a bullet hit him in the forehead. He collapsed on to the ground face up. The men around him stalled and one by one died.

The Silencer heard Reynold's attack and looked at Cody, "Charge"

Cody and his men stood up and began their fatal charge.

The Silencer looked on. *This is over. Well, at least I can kill one of the Schneiders.* He raised his pistol and took aim at Cody. Slowly squeezing the trigger, he fired. As Cody was running, a dead man lurched into his right shoulder. His body spun just as a bullet struck his left shoulder, throwing him down. Writhing in pain, he got to his knees just as two bodies fell on top of him.

The battle was over. What seemed like hours to each side was really a matter of minutes. Could you call it a battle? Cody would say later, "It was a Crime."

The Silencer stood far behind his men. Turning, he

walked away and disappeared into the shadows of the woods. The books still were the key to his success. *One way or another I will get them.* Thinking to himself, he smiled.

The screaming, the chaos and then the worst part; the silence. The Muddville 'Militia' stood up. This was the first time any of them had taken a human life. Even though they were defending their hometown, it shook them. Down below in the ravine was a line of dead bodies. The line where they could go no farther. Sid remembers calling it 'The Deadline.' The Sheriff sent most of the men back to the town just in case there was another attack.

Sid stared at the devastation, tears in his eyes, saying, "They are my enemies, yet my heart bleeds for them."

Cody

CHAPTER 22

CODY'S RESCUE

As Cody recalls, "I was stuck, I could not move. My shoulder was on fire. Warm blood was dripping on my face and eyes. Every moment felt like it was going to be my last one. Then suddenly there came a silence. *What was happening?* I tried to move. Nothing. I tried again and I saw a little bit of daylight."

At that same moment Sid began to walk through the carnage, looking at the mangled mess of the bodies. The question arose, *"Would the Collective come back to take care of their dead or would the Muddville people have to do it?"* Staring at the 'Deadline,' he saw two young boys holding hands as they died. Sid's heart sunk even further. The boys were twins. Somehow, they had found each other in the heat of battle right before death. *What would their mother think?* Suddenly one of the bodies moved. Sid looked closer. No, it was something under the bodies. Rolling the one twin to the left, he looked down into the blinking eyes of a young man. Sid looked around. No one was watching. "Here let me help you out." Helping Cody get out from underneath the twins and other fallen bodies, he stood him up. The boy seemed dazed. Supporting Cody, Sid said, "Come on, let's get you out of here." Walking as fast as Cody could, they made it to the tree line. Skirting the tree line, Sid led the young man away from the battlefield. "I know an abandoned house I use sometimes, it's just on the outskirts of town. I'll take you there to recover. We'll figure out what to do with you later."

Cody said nothing. They walked along the row of trees. They reached the house which was surrounded by some woods. Sid looked around. No one followed. Hopefully, no one saw them. "In here." They went inside the small house. "Rather musty, I'm sorry." They sat down and Sid looked at the young man. "What's your name?"

Ever so quietly he said, "Cody."

Sid knelt. "Let's take a look at that shoulder." Peering at the wound, he said "The bullet is still in there. This might hurt." Sid poured some alcohol on the open wound.

Cody screamed.

Sid stood up. "You'll be ok for the time being. I'm going to get the doctor."

An hour later, Sid returned with a tall man with a beard. He was wearing glasses. A boy followed Sid into the room. "This is Doc Klingaman and my friend Brucie." Sid announced.

Brucie just stared at Cody, "Is he really Collective?"

Sid laughed, "Now, now, he's just like me and you. Can you fix him doc?"

The Doctor opened his black bag. "It's going to hurt. I will need both of you to hold him down.

Sid held Cody's shoulders down and Brucie took ahold of his free hand. The doctor looked down on Cody. "Bite down on this rag." Cody bit down, eyes wide open. Doc Klingaman began to dig with a knife. Pain shot through Cody's body and he groaned and bit down even harder. Brucie screamed "He's breaking my hand! Don't squeeze so hard!" Cody passed out. Doc Klingaman finally pried the bullet out.

Sometime later, Cody looked up into the Doctor's eyes.

"You're lucky young feller. You'll heal just fine." Turning, the doctor began to pack his bag.

Sid walked over to the doctor, "I think it would be best if we said nothing about this to anyone."

"Yes, yes." The doctor fastened his bag, "Doctor's oath, remember?"

Sid nodded and walked the doctor to the door. "Thanks Doc!" he said.

The doctor paused at the door and turned looking at Cody, "It's a strange thing. By the looks of your wound You were shot by one of your own men."

Cody just stared. *Who?*

Sid smiled and walked back to Cody. "Well Cody, I think it's best if you stay here for a while until you heal. I'm not sure how the town's people would tolerate a stranger. Shoot, they barely tolerate me. I'll get you some food. Brucie and I will drop it by every now and then." Cody nodded, still in shock. "Remember, my name is Sid, and this is Brucie. And what are you going to do?"

The reply came, "Stay put."

"Well then, I'm off. See you later." The two walked out the door. Cody laid down and shut his eyes. His head spun and the death screams came back to him loudly.

What now? Where was Kim?

THE ADVENTURE
BEGINS

Kim

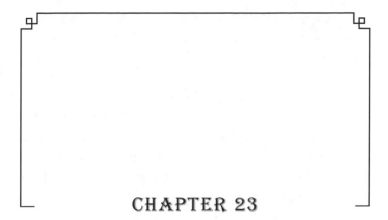

CHAPTER 23

KIM'S ASSIGNMENT

Kim's favorite place was the corner of her apartment where she did her yoga. Slowly, she worked her way into a handstand and remained silent for several minutes. She was feeling proud of her run today. Kim had run outside on the trails in the hills outside of the Collective. Trail running had become her second favorite time, being outside and free. Next, there was her martial arts training. Kim walked into the room and was surprised to see Talon with her little group. She was leading the training exercise. Kim had not seen them for days.

Talon had brought her team back in for some rest and to debrief with the Controller. She liked running the training session.

"Attention!" A large screen descended in the front of the room. This was a daily occurrence throughout the Collective. The Controller appeared on the screen. "Let us now say the pledge." All over the Collective, old, and young people began to recite their vow to the Collective.

"I pledge my allegiance to the Collective, for the good of the people. May I wither and die if I doubt any part of the one true Collective. I will render obedience to the Controller of the Collective, fulfilling my duties of the people and for the people. May the glory of the Collective live forever."

As the screen ascended, Talon barked, "Everyone in plank position. Let's see how long you can hold it." Kim focused on her breathing.

Thirty seconds and the whole group was still planking. It was not only Talon's group. All off duty security forces were required to attend the session.

One minute. One or two people dropped out. Kim smiled to herself. She had been practicing.

Ninety seconds. A few more dropped out

Two minutes. Ten people were left. Kim again focused on her breathing.

Seconds ticked away, closing in on three minutes. Kim and Manon were the last ones left.

Talon announced, "Our two winners. It's only fitting that they have a sparring match to break the tie."

Slowly, the two girls stood and faced each other. The rest of the room circled around them.

Manon closed the gap and threw a stinging left jab to Kim's face. Kim's head spun. Lightheaded, Kim threw her own jab as Manon countered another hard punch.

Kim circled and danced away. The room was a bit fuzzy.

The two began to circle each other, trading jabs as Kim's head began to clear.

Kim threw a hard punch followed by a second, which drove Manon backward.

They circled, trading punches, and blocking each other.

Manon went low with a punch to the stomach, making Kim gasp. Kim countered with a right and left hit to Manon's face.

Manon backed up and began to circle again. Pure hatred filled her eyes as she stared at Kim. *How many times had they been pitted against each other?* Continuing to circle, each looked for an opening.

Manon attacked with a shot to the body and then to the face. Kim countered with a stinging jab to the nose.

Manon threw a hook that just missed over the top. Kim ducked away.

Kim launched her first real attack with a series of jabs to the body and then up to the head.

Manon stumbled backwards, gasping for air. Kim pressed forward, only to be met with three jabs to the face and one to the gut.

Circling, Manon attacked with an upper cut to Kim's chin. Retreating a little late, she got hit with another left. Kim countered with a crushing punch to the body and then danced away, throwing a series of jabs.

Manon charged, but couldn't find the range as Kim circled. Blocking one of Manon's jabs, Kim countered with two stunning blows to the face. Manon countered with her own two.

Manon charged again, only to be met with a solid punch to the face. Kim began a series of jabs and then landed another punch to the face. She finished with a second crushing punch to the nose.

Talon screamed, "Stop!"

A man walked into the room. "Ma'am?"

Talon turned, "What do you want?"

The soldier stiffened, "Ma'am, the Controller wants to see you and Miss Schneider."

Manon spit blood out of her mouth. "I had you."

Kim turned and followed Talon as she marched out of the room. *That didn't need a response.*

Kim tried to compose herself. *Clear the mind. Clear the mind. They have ways to read the mind.* The Collective had a scientific division that monitored all the thoughts of the people inside. Promoting the good vision of the good people and catching any of the bad. One of the jobs of the security forces was to catch the doubters. Really, that was the Silencer's job. *If she held her mind with no thoughts, they couldn't track it.* She should know. She herself had used the methods and developed mind control. They would be watching all her thoughts and emotions. The only way to make it safe was to make your mind a blank.

They approached the Controller's office. There was a guard on each side of the door. The soldier to the left responded, "You two are expected." Opening the door to a huge ornate office, Kim stepped in. The door shut quickly behind her, leaving her facing a man sifting through a mass of papers on his desk. He had a dark complexion, sporting a short, well-trimmed mustache. The Controller wore the traditional black shirt and tie with a black suit coat. She was still in her workout gear, showing off her perfect muscular body. Sweat began to drip as she waited for the Controller to speak. Still no response. She wiped a drop of sweat off her nose.

The Controller looked up. "Ah, Miss Schneider, you and Talon are here." A tall man, he gave her a smile. *A politician's smile*, Kim thought. The smile brought out the wrinkles in the corners of his eyes. He went back to straightening his desk.

Talon walked over to the left of the Controller's desk and remained with her hood pulled up. Kim watched Talon. She was stunning, with beautiful black hair and jet-black eyes. Those eyes that caught you, trapping you, evoking a hypnotic power over you. As Kim looked deep into those eyes, she also noticed unusual flecks of gold. Talon had a powerful presence in the room. A slow smile appeared but quickly faded as she stepped in closer, looking down on Kim. The inspection over, she stepped back. "I trained this one, you know." The Controller nodded.

She continued, "I see you are training well young lady. I hear that you are in search of a hand to hand combat attack that there is no defense for." She laughed, and that chilled Kim to her bones. "Fool! There is no such attack. Give up your search. It is a waste of your time."

"Enough!" The Controller broke in. "Miss Schneider, you know Talon."

Suddenly, from the right side of the desk, a woman stepped forward. She was wearing a white blouse. Her slacks were a mustard-color. Beautiful. Her purple hair was brushed up high and over to the right in a unique style. *How had she missed her*? Kim felt something was off. The lady's smile seemed not quite real. How had she been next to the Controller and gone unnoticed? Kim studied the lady.

Stepping to Kim, she held out her hand and shook Kim's. The Controller introduced the lady. "Miss Schneider, this is my top advisor, Lexa."

Lexa smiled, "An honor to meet you. We have high hopes for you and your future."

The Controller turned to Kim. "I, we, the Collective needs your help. First, the Collective wants you to go out and find your brother Cody. He's been in a battle."

"NO!" Shouted Talon, "No battle. Just a little skirmish."

The Controller continued, "Quite right, more of a nuisance really. We need to talk to him, no harm, no foul. You understand, right Kim?" Way deep in the back of Kim's mind an image appeared. She fought to keep it back. *Yeah right. She had a vivid image of her sister being tortured. All the blood. Her sister's last words, "Tell them I love them."*

Kim's eyes teared up. Lucky her eyes were a little puffy from the fight and sweat was dripping all over the place. No one noticed.

The Controller continued, "More importantly, I need you to find two men: Dan Shoop and Sid Finch. Shoop is really our troublemaker. You see, he has written the history of the world. The Finch fellow is a newspaper man. You must destroy any written word about the Collective, especially Shoop's book. Whatever he has. The two men? Well, do what you want. Bring them back or…."

Talon hissed, "Kill them."

Lexa stepped forward, "You see, no written record must exist of the Collective. The outside world must not know about us. At the same time, the people in the conscious Collective must not know about the outsiders. That knowledge has gotten out and caused our current problems. You must tell no one inside or outside of the Collective what you're doing."

The Controller finished. "You must leave as soon as

possible. All contact information will be given to you. Start your search in Muddville. That is where Shoop was last seen."

Kim saluted and turned to leave.

Talon coolly said, "Remember child, I will be watching every move you make."

Kim walked back to her apartment among the crowds of people. Safe here among all the other thoughts. *What has Cody gotten into? A week ago, he had said he was with the Silencer and that they were going to fight someone. His exact statement was 'I am going to battle'. Why did the Controller cover it up? Where was the Silencer? He could not be trusted at all. She had not seen him in days. He was nowhere, as though he had not existed.*

Can I find Cody?

CHAPTER 24

TAKING CARE OF PROBLEMS

After Kim had left the meeting, the Controller looked at Lexa and Talon. "Take a seat. We need to discuss our real problem." Leading Talon and Lexa over to a conference table, they sat down. Lexa began, "In my mind the problem to be dealt with first and foremost is information. We can't allow any people to have it."

The Controller looked over at Talon. "She's already been working on that end. Silencing any outsiders that are storytellers, musicians, or artists. The book or books that Dan Shoop wrote about the true history of the world must be destroyed. That is paramount. That is part of the reason I sent Kim out there."

Talon glared at Lexa, "What about the townspeople that will talk after the fiasco that the Silencer has gotten us into?"

Lexa smiled politely back at Talon, "Well, for my part, I am going to reinstate a new curriculum in Muddville's education. Then add some terrible rumors about you to the local people. We will indoctrinate the young. Then scare the old so badly that they will run and hide. Eventually, someday, the young will then join the Collective."

Talon inquired, "And those that don't conform?"

"We'll take care of them later," was the response.

The debate between the two ladies continued.

"What about Kim, can she be trusted?"

"She'll be fine." Lexa defended.

"I doubt it," Talon sneered.

The Controller stopped the escalation of words. "Talon, you need to take care of our first problem. The Silencer! The fool must be dealt with immediately. How you do it, well, that's up to you. You are the only one that can handle the Silencer." This brought a smile to Talon's face. Looking over at Lexa, the Controller said, "I expect to hear some good news from your end soon."

Both ladies left smiling, but they did not walk out of the office together. Lexa turned to the left to go to her office as Talon was joined by four of her people. *Interesting,* Lexa thought, *in the past Talon has always had five people with her.* She overheard one man say, "Where to now?"

"Back outside." Came the reply.

As Talon's group left the Collective and made their way to their camp, she said "We're going to start infiltrating the town. Same rules apply, take nothing and stay out of sight."

In unison, "Yes Ma'am."

Turning to Manon, "I want you to follow Kim Schneider, and if you catch her alone, kill her!"

Alice was excited and giddy when she heard that. "Can I go?"

"NO! You're with me."

Manon said nothing. Her eye was beginning to turn black from one of Kim's punches.

Grandma Miller

CHAPTER 25

KIM

K im sat alone in her apartment, considering her latest assignment as she packed to leave for Muddville. *She had been alone and away from her family during her early training with the security forces. Alone and afraid, not getting to see her family was the worst. Talon saw the loneliness and had taken Kim under her wing back then. Remembering Talon's friendship was a double-edged sword. The woman could be nice and cruel at the same time. Had she really been nice or was it a trick? Going through the training, she was always in fear of Talon's temper tantrums. Now, as she reflected on the way Talon looked at her in the meeting, she wasn't so sure what to think about her. School had been easy, and after the training, being in the Security team was routine. She enjoyed working out; it gave her some much- needed confidence. This was her first real assignment. Alone again and on my own,* she thought. *She had lucked into a promotion because the*

Silencer had assumed that she had caught her sister Kelly. That fact weighed heavy on her mind. Maybe she had moved up the ladder too fast.

Life so far had been controlled and protected by her parents. Especially her father, who had given her guidance along the way. Kim had always been able to ask her father about problems that she had been confronted with. Recalling back, *'Pops, what do you think?' He had always given her advice, while allowing her the freedom to do what she wanted. Then, too, were the teachers that had structured her life. Even the Silencer and Talon had guided her through the training. Now, to think, traveling on the outside on your own. She would miss her father the most.* Kim finished her preparations to leave. *Was this a good thing?* She had tears in her eyes and butterflies in her stomach. She locked her apartment door. *Maybe for the last time,* she thought. She moved to the exit point of the Collective.

At the same moment, Manon was packing her things. She had reentered the Collective to follow Kim. To kill Kim would be nice. Kim had always bragged about her family. For Manon, who had no family, that was a hard pill to swallow. Thinking back over the last couple of weeks with Talon, she had found she liked the freedom of the outside world for some reason. Manon had told no one these thoughts. Finishing her packing, she walked to the exit point.

The guard inside the Collective would notify the guards on the outside. They would wake her body up on the outside and disconnect all the tubes and wires. Manon sat up and walked to a corner of the building where she couldn't be seen. It was not a long wait. She saw Kim sit up and begin to move.

Manon rose slowly, then at a safe distance followed Kim to the exit point.

Kim paused. Standing there looking out at the unknown. Taking the first step outside of the Collective was the hardest. *Look around and enjoy nature*, she told herself. Traveling down the dusty road, she headed out. Kim was amazed at the variety this world had. Inside the Collective the world seemed so uniform compared to this one.

Manon was thinking this could be it. I can get her now! She moved closer and then suddenly, Kim stopped.

After an hour Kim spied a man and a woman talking by a farmhouse. She approached them. Getting her courage up she asked, "Could you tell me how to get to Muddville?"

"Why sure," the man replied. "I'm going that way myself; I'll walk you there." Looking at the lady and laughing, "Got to earn my wings some way."

Kim took off in a southernly direction with her newfound friend.

"I'm Kim," she said, reaching out her hand.

"I'm Bret," and they shook hands. Bret looked at her, "You know, you look like a girl that used to hang out in Muddville. Kelly, I believe her name was." Kim did not respond as they moved forward. Along the way Kim began to see the buildings of a small town off in the distance. "Is that Muddville?" she asked. "Yes, it sure is." Bret replied, and then inquired. "What brings you to Muddville?"

"Well, I'm looking for a man named Dan Shoop."

"Ah. The history teacher, a good man. My kids loved his class. You will need to talk to Superintendent Jake Allen. He will be able to point you in the right direction. Ask around town for him. He is a big man with a hardy laugh. Well, here's where we part company; my home is just over to the east a bit." Pointing west, "there is the main drag into town."

Kim thanked Bret and headed towards her first destination. Walking among the small, quaint houses she spotted a sign: Rooms for Rent. This will be great. Knocking on the door of the house an old lady answered. She was small in stature, with white curly hair and glasses. "Hello, young lady. How can I help you?"

Kim smiled, "I would like a room if I may."

"You may indeed. My name is Mrs. Miller." She handed Kim a paper. "Here are the rules of my house, sign right there and you're good to go." Kim entered the house and was shown to her room.

"I think I am going to walk around town a bit, Mrs. Miller and then I'll be back."

"Why, you can call me Grandma, everyone does. Have a good time dear," said Mrs. Miller.

Kim located the school and then found the Sheriff's office, which was down from Pat's tavern. She made her way back to Mrs. Miller's house, exploring some of the back alleys. That night she enjoyed a home cooked meal. The old woman talked her leg off. What was she doing here? Where was she going? On and on. Kim fielded most of the questions as politely as she could. Up in her room that night, she went over the day's events. A good start all in all.

The hunt for Dan Shoop starts tomorrow.

CHAPTER 26

THE CELEBRATION

A week after the battle, Muddville held its annual celebration. There was a lot to be thankful for this year. The town had grown, and the farmers were doing well. Winning the battle added to the excitement. Contests of all kinds were held, with both the winners and losers enjoying themselves. It was one big party for the community.

The people came out in droves to enjoy the sunny day. Families old and young came to the park grounds to be entertained. Kim sat with Grandma Miller at the pie judging tent. She had eaten too much. She was experimenting with every different food she could find. Too many sweets! Sitting there she felt a little sick. She had spent four days exploring the town and getting to know the people. Next week she would try to find Dan Shoop.

Deep inside a fortune teller's tent, Manon watched Kim. *Kim had too many people around her*, Manon thought. *Be patient, your time will come.* She too had experimented at this fair. Manon now sported a lion tattoo on her left shoulder. She smiled as she looked down at it. It had been bold of her to experiment with this tattoo. It had taken two hours for the tattoo artist to complete the lion. Now all she had to do was hide it from Talon. *Who knows what she would think?*

Talon also had a spot on a hill overlooking the park. She stood in the middle of some trees to watch the town. Jesse and Frank had been sent to snoop around the town while all the people were at the park.

An announcer bellowed out. "Ladies and gentlemen, come one come all!" The crowd began to gather around a small table. Pointing to one side of the circle. "We have here, the almighty Jake Allen, the Superintendent of our schools." A cheer went up from the crowd as Jake stepped forward. Turning to the other side of the circle, the announcer said, "And here we have Sheriff James, the winner of Muddville's first battle." A roar arose as James stepped forward.

A woman in overalls stepped in close to the contestants. She tucked her purple hair inside of her scarf.

No one noticed.

The men positioned themselves at the table. The announcer continued, "It is time for the arm-wrestling championship contest." The crowd cheered again. Jake and James clasped hands, staring at each other intently. The hands were bound in a way to give neither an advantage.

James snarled, "Loser, you're mine."

The judge stepped forward. Looking at both men. "Are you ready?" Both nodded.

"Begin."

For a good thirty seconds there was no movement. The

crowd held their breath as the two men's faces became red. Slowly, ever so slowly, James began to take the advantage inch by inch. Just as it looked like James would triumph, with a herculean effort Jake evened the match. He brought their hands back to the starting position. His supporters cheered. Again, Sheriff James moved the hands back in favor of himself. Jake's hand was three inches from defeat. There, the two men stayed locked for what seemed like forever. Sheriff James gave a mighty grunt and Jake's hand hit the table.

The announcer's voice could barely be heard over the cheers of the crowd. "Our very own Muddville champion!"

The two men stood up and shook hands as Jake raised James's hand high in the air.

James laughed, "See Jake, I got Shoop's lesson after all. Look at what I've become!"

Jake smiled, "Ah, James my poor boy. I just don't want to be king of Muddville. I want to have the best school in the country."

Turning, Jake was hugged by his wife. "You did good, Honey, I'm proud of you," she said.

As Jake and his wife walked off together, he said, "I mean it. I want to run the best school system in the country. The world! Why not? Now I must figure out how!"

CHAPTER 27

A MEETING WITH JAKE ALLEN

A few days later in Muddville, Jake Allen's secretary escorted Lexa into his office. Lexa sat down in front of Jake. She turned to the secretary, "Thanks so much, you can go now." Karen frowned as she left thinking *Who does she think she is?* The conversation began. It was one-sided, with Lexa doing all the talking.

"Do I get a thank you?"

"Yes, yes of course," said Jake.

"I am going to help you again." Jake raised his eyebrows. Producing a large volume of materials, Lexa dropped them on his desk. "Here is your new school curriculum. A detailed way to run your school and even Muddville itself. You do control the town, do you not?"

Jake stammered "Well, kind of." In the back of Jake's

mind, he thought. *He could control the school board, but the town council might cause him some problems. A town council that had closed minds and didn't like change.* His attention snapped back to Lexa.

Lexa continued, "If you follow this detailed program, you will have the best town and school in the country. People will want to come here to learn from you and imitate your success."

Jake looked Lexa over, "And if I choose not to?"

"Then quite simply, I will take this somewhere else and you will fail. People will leave. The town will wither and die. Your choice or not." Adding, "One more thing, you choose now. If I walk out, the deal is off. Oh! Remember you already owe me."

Jakes mind floated back to Sheriff James being happy with his title 'King of Muddville.' He himself wanted more. His favorite uncle had always challenged him to strive for more. To be the best. Jake looked at the woman. There was that smile again, Jake winced. Taking in a deep breath, he said "Okay, I'll do it."

Lexa stood up and as she left the room she turned, "It starts today. You must execute every detail, or the deal is off."

"Wait, what's your name? Where did you come from?"

She was already outside, "Not important" came the reply.

That afternoon, people began to stroll into Pat's tavern after work. A lady walked into the bar. She had a short purple hair cut. Sitting down among the regulars, she ordered a drink. When the bartender brought her the drink. She asked him if he had seen a little blonde that was asking after the history teacher.

"Shoop? No, Ma'am."

Lexa sat pleasantly waiting, listening to the people. The talk was of the day's work and complaints about bosses. Soon discussions went into stories about the battle. Some young people were excited, others felt bad about the killing. One young fellow said, "Do you think they will want revenge?" Lexa raised her voice, saying "I heard there is someone dressed in black killing families outside of town." The crowd got quiet.

"No way that's true."

"Yep, I heard that story from someone else."

Another man added, "They're killing storytellers, artists and writers."

And it went on, one story after another. Lexa got up and walked out, leaving the rumor mill in high pitch. Smiling, she thought *Muddville people would either shut up to save their families or they would leave town and hide. Job done!* and she smiled again. *A well-executed plan.*

The bartender looked up. "Hey! where'd that lady go? She didn't finish her drink."

CHAPTER 28

JAKE ALLEN'S BUSY DAY

Lexa entered Muddville wearing a more conservative outfit then she had worn on her first visit to the town. She explored the town in an attempt to learn as much about these people as she could. She stopped to talk to the old lady she had met tending her flowers. Lexa then headed back to the Collective, satisfied that she had learned as much as she could.

Earlier that morning Kim had woken up and she too was walking around town. Getting up her courage, she entered the Superintendent's office only to be told that he had a terribly busy day. There might be a chance late in the afternoon to see him. Kim turned away, discouraged.

Jake Allen came into the Superintendent's office. He stood looking at the high school across the street. Summer break had just started. Sipping his coffee, he wondered how the day would go.

"You have a full day, Sir" the Secretary said.

"Yes, you're right. A lot to do and most of it unpleasant." He gave a deep sigh, "Well Karen, let's get started." Walking down the hallway to his office, he sat down and flipped back through the curriculum he'd been given. Jake had stayed up late the night before to study what must be done. *Would this really get him the school system that he wanted?* Reflecting on the next couple of meetings, he thought *Change is difficult, but one must look at the bigger picture to see the good that will come of it. I, no we, will build a better school and a better town.*

One by one teachers were called in, given new assignments, or weeded out.

"Mr. Shoop to see you, sir," the secretary announced.

Jake swallowed hard. *This would be the most difficult one.* Dan Shoop had been one of his favorite teachers.

Jake started out, "I'm sorry to inform you that your services are no longer needed." Dan Shoop stared at Jake in disbelief.

"No History? No position for a veteran teacher? No loyalty to years of service?"

"There is a new curriculum, and quite frankly, you, Sir, are not a part of it. I'm sorry. I need younger teachers that have new ideas. This will be the new age of Muddville."

Shoop shook his head, "You mean new teachers that you can fit into your mold."

Jake forced a smile, "I'm sorry. The decision has already been made. Mr. Shoop, you have a nice day." Dan Shoop turned and left, marching out of the Superintendent's office. *Somehow, some way the Collective was behind all this.*

Dan stepped outside into the sunlight. Looking up he saw his new friend, Sid Finch, walking towards him. Muttering, as they passed each other. "Bad things are happening, I told you so." Sid watched his friend walk away. Turning back, he entered the reception area and introduced himself to the Secretary. "I am Sid Finch. May I say you look very pretty today." Spying the name plate on her desk he added, "Karen."

She smiled at him. "Please wait here while I tell Mr. Allen you have arrived."

Moments later, Sid was escorted into Jake's office. "You wanted to talk to me, Mr. Allen?"

Jake turned, finishing off his third cup of coffee. "Quite right. You are relatively new to Muddville Mr. Finch. I'm sorry to inform you that the town council wants no more newspaper."

Jake thought to himself. *He had pulled a lot of strings and asked for a few favors to get three of the council members to go his way. Just enough for the board to accept his plan.*

Sid stood aghast. "You're kidding, right?"

"No sir, I am not kidding. The office space is yours to do with what you want. We want no more newspaper. Sir, I am sorry, but I have a busy schedule. Please see yourself out. Good day." Jake gave a brief smile and called the secretary to bring in the next person.

Sid Finch had done a lot of travelling in his life and had begun thinking *this just might be home. Wrong. Muddville had just become another stop. What do I do with Brucie? Maybe I can find another job here. Life was getting complicated. I should talk to Shoop, but he looked mad when we passed each other.*

Jake's day passed quickly. The meetings were not

all bad. People were excited about promotions and new teaching assignments. Math and English departments were given higher status over all other subjects, so they were the happiest. The meetings were almost over as Jake sat at his desk contemplating the future. Leaning back in his chair, he was finally able to relax.

"Sir." Karen stuck her head in Jake's office. "There's a young lady here to see you." Jake looked up. "Are there any more meetings?"

"No sir," came the reply.

Jake sat up. "Very well, send her in."

Kim walked into the office. Not as big or grand as the Controller's office she thought. Introducing herself, "I am Kim Schneider. I need your help."

"And what would that be?" Jake smiled.

Stammering Kim asked, "I would like to talk to one of your teachers, Dan Shoop."

He laughed, "Bad luck young lady, he is not with us anymore. We released him this morning. I don't think he'll be staying around town much more either. I'm sorry."

Kim dropped her head. Her heart sunk and she sighed. "Thank you for your time." Turning slowly, she walked out. *"Now, what do I do?"*

Kim stepped outside as Jake yelled, "Hey, Miss Schneider, you might try the tavern. I've seen him there on some nights with another man named Sid Finch." The spring in her step was back. Not only was she close to Shoop she had also located Finch. Truly her lucky day.

Moments later, Kim entered the tavern. It was early afternoon when she walked into Pat's. The bartender looked up. "Can I help you?"

Kim looked around observing. "Not many people in here."

"Can I get you a drink?" said the man.

"Well, maybe some water. I'm hoping to see Dan Shoop here." The water was set in front of Kim.

The bartender began to explain, "People usually come here after dinner or sometimes after lunch. Mostly dinner. Shoop's been here a couple of nights. You see, part of my problem is there was a strange lady in here the other day spreading rumors. People are kind of edgy now."

"What did she look like?" Kim asked. "Did she have black hair?" *Was Talon here?*

He shook his head, "No, tall with a short haircut. Her hair was purple. I haven't ever seen that color of hair. As a matter of fact, she asked about you." Kim sat stunned. She only knew one person fitting that description. *Could it be?*

Why would Lexa try to hunt her down? *Talon hated her. Did Lexa hate her too? Were they working together? Did the Controller set her up to fail?* Kim's head began to spin, creating dark thoughts.

The bartender continued, "Shoop? I don't know. He's not a regular. You'll just have to come back later in the evening and see for yourself." Kim took a long drink of her water. The bartender wiped his bar down. "Dan Shoop was my kid's teacher. They loved his class."

Kim smiled and said goodbye. She headed back to Grandma's house. Better get some rest now as she might be up late tonight. At dinner, Kim told Grandma what she was doing. "You see, I'm trying to find Dan Shoop. He's got a book that I'd like to read. I have some friends that like history and would like to read it as well. I've heard that he goes to Pat's Tavern some evenings. I decided that's where

I'm going tonight to see if I can find him. Could you leave the back door unlocked? I might be up late tonight."

The old lady smiled, shaking her finger at Kim. "Be careful young lady, there's a bad element in that tavern. I hope you find Dan." Kim nodded. Grandma added, "I will leave a treat for you when you get back."

The sun was setting as Kim walked down the back alleys. Finding the rear door to Pat's, she edged her way in. The hallway was unlit, and the floor was sticky from spilt beer. She had figured that coming in from the alley would be the best way to enter unseen. Finding a table in the darkest corner, with almost no light, she settled in. *Maybe she could really be a spy for the Collective after all.*

Kim at Pat's Tavern

CHAPTER 29

A NIGHT AT PAT'S

Kim sat at a small table away from the crowd. She pulled the ball cap she had found low over her eyes, a trick she'd learned in her training with Talon. She had always emphasized hiding your eyes from people. If you made no eye contact, the people would never know that you were there. Sitting there watching people, she learned a lot about the locals. They were joking and complaining about work. Pat's was a place to release the stress and pressures of the day. They were normal people. There was really no difference from the people in the Collective. Wake up, go to work, come home. Every day was exactly the same. Kim was finishing off her second glass of water when she saw two men enter the bar.

Unbeknownst to Kim, Manon sat in the opposite corner of the bar, behind a large group of people. She had proudly rolled up her shirt sleeve so her new lion tattoo was visible. Her sole focus was to watch Kim and try to catch her alone.

The crowd at the bar called the two men over. "Damn, Shoop, I heard they fired you today. Crazy, right? You're the best teacher in the building."

Shoop looked at the man. "Was. Was the best. Just a bad day, boys. Hope you all don't have one like I had."

Another man turned and looked at the long-haired man. "So, Sid I hear they are closing the newspaper. A sad day for Muddville. Tell you what barkeep, I got the first round for these two." The bartender nodded. Pouring two beers, he handed Dan and Sid each a glass. Thanking the man, they walked back to a table away from the crowd. Kim sat still. She wasn't that close to the men, yet she could barely hear, at least when the crowd wasn't too loud.

"What are you going to do?" Sid asked.

Kim was making mental notes. *Sid Finch: five foot seven inches, maybe, long white hair with a long white mustache. He wore sunglasses but only took them off once he sat down in the dark room. Dan Shoop, a smaller man, five feet four inches maybe. Light red hair and wire-rimmed glasses.*

Shoop replied, "Most of my stuff is at my house in the woods. I need to clean out my classroom. I also need to go to the library and finish my research."

Sid shook his head, "You and your research."

Shoop leaned forward. "Look, there's been someone following me. Can't tell who, they wear a black hood." Adding, "I should have left with Billy and Kelly."

Kim stiffened at the name of her sister. She had not known what had happened to her sister. This was good news. Kelly was alive!

Shoop looked at Sid, "What are you going to do?"

Sid shrugged, "Not sure… maybe a new job? Life's not all about me anymore. It has gotten complicated. I need to take care of Brucie and…." Sid drifted off.

"What? What is it you're not telling me?" Dan asked.

"Dan, I walked through the battlefield after the fight, and I found a young man from the Collective still alive. I rescued one of the Collective's soldiers!" Sid stammered, "Can you believe it? His name is Cody."

Shoop sat in shock. "You saved a man from the Collective? Sid what were you thinking? Turn him in to the Sheriff. There might be a reward for the man."

"I just had to help someone in need," Sid explained. "The guy needed my help. He doesn't talk much. He is still in shock. He was shot. He's healing but has really bad dreams about the battle."

Kim gasped. The two men looked around. Kim remained unseen for the moment, dropping her head. She pulled the ball cap lower. Shoop stood up. "Sorry my friend, I must leave. If you want to talk to me again, I'll be at my house." Dan left Pat's Tavern that night for the last time. Sid stood up and moved to the bar to talk to some people. "Another beer here, please."

Kim's mind was on how to find Dan Shoop. Could she find his house out in the woods? Maybe if she found his house and waited until he left, she could steal the book.

Shoop was gone. Sid's back was turned. It was time to leave. Kim left Pat's with a crowd of people and headed back to Grandma's house. *It was all too much to process. She had found Finch and Shoop, but it sounded like they may not be here for long. Could she find Dan Shoop's house? That was the key. Wow. Talon was out there somewhere and so was Lexa. Why? She had heard the men talk about her sister Kelly. Now she knew that her brother Cody was alive as well. Her family! What would her father do?*

Manon followed Kim out of the bar. She was close enough to hear her muttering to herself "I must find Dan Shoop's house tomorrow." Kim turned down a street and was alone. Manon closed the gap. Her hand lifted her knife from her belt. Suddenly, Kim turned into a yard. Manon backed away just as an old lady opened the door to the house. "There you are, darling."

Kim stepped inside the house. "You waited up for me."

"I sure did!" The old lady closed the door as Manon watched from the shadows.

Grandma handed Kim some cookies and a glass of milk. "Here you go. Off to bed with you. Pleasant dreams."

Kim took the homemade goodies to her room. Sitting on the edge of the bed, eating her cookies, she mulled over the day's events. *What was more important, retrieving Shoop's book or saving her family? The Collective was becoming less and less trustworthy in her mind.* Sleep did not come for a long, long time that night. Her brother and sister were out there somewhere. Her eyes began to tear up. Drying her eyes with her sleeve she wondered what she was going to do.

Meanwhile, Manon watched the house for a while then slowly moved off to find a place to sleep. Wondering if Kim was going to that house tomorrow. She would have to follow her. Killing Kim and the historian. That would be a double bonus.

Manon

CHAPTER 30

THE FIGHT

Manon was up early the next morning. She began by going to the bakery and asking the baker where Dan Shoop's house was.

The baker rubbed his chin, "If I recall, he lives west of here in a big forest."

Manon got a doughnut and tried to remember the maps that Talon had made during all those days scouting the areas around Muddville. Just before she turned to leave, the baker stopped her.

"Sheriff James will be in here in a few minutes to get his morning coffee." Pointing at a chair, "Why don't you wait over there and when he comes in you can ask him for directions yourself."

Manon sat down, finishing off her doughnut. Licking her lips, she thought, *another good thing about this outside world. She had no memories of a family like Kim had. Why?*

Her mind snapped back, thinking about Talon's map. West, more woods, and fields. Less people. That would be good for her to gain an advantage over Kim.

Sheriff James entered as the baker came out from the back. He handed the Sheriff a cup of coffee with steam rolling off the top of the cup. "Good Morning Sheriff." Nodding towards Manon, "That girl needs a map to Dan Shoop's house."

The Sheriff eyed Manon. "Well it is the weekend; he'll probably be home."

The baker chimed in. "He got fired the other day. It might not be his home much longer."

"Ah! Right you are." Sitting down next to Manon, the sheriff began to draw a crude map. Manon laughed to herself. *Talon's maps were much better.*

Manon took the map, "Thank you, Sir." Smiling at the big man with her best smile, she left the bakery and headed back to the house where she had last seen Kim.

As Kim was finishing up breakfast she explained, "I'm going out to Dan Shoop's House today."

Taking Kim's dishes, the old lady said, "Okay, you be careful."

Kim packed a sandwich and some water as doubts began to fill her mind. *Could she find the place? That Finch guy had her brother. How could she save him?*

Leaving Grandma's house, Kim headed to the Sherriff's office. She walked down the street, unaware that Manon was following. Soon she saw the office. Opening the door, she entered. Sitting at his desk, Sheriff James was drinking his coffee.

He smiled, "You're the one staying at Granny's house."

Kim returned the smile, "Yes, sir. Could you do me a favor and draw me a map to Dan Shoop's house? I want to talk to him about his history book."

The Sheriff pulled out a piece of paper and began to draw. "You know you're the second person today asking me for this map."

Kim's mouth dropped, "Who?"

"Don't know. I've never seen her before." James handed the map to Kim. "Have a safe trip. I got things to do." They both headed for the door.

Kim headed west with the sun on her back. Houses began to vanish as she headed down a broken-down, dusty road. A road that seemed to go nowhere. *Had Talon or Lexa asked for the map?*

Manon had started her tail far behind Kim. Over time, she began slowly closing the gap. Suddenly, Kim stopped and sat on a rock under a tree to rest. She took out some water and drank from the bottle. As Manon watched Kim from her hiding place, she thought to herself *'Weakling.'* Waiting for Kim to continue her journey, Manon took out her knife and began to sharpen the blade. *This place was out in broad daylight. Not good for an attack here. Wait and be patient.*

Kim looked up at the sun. The Sheriff had said it was a good hour and a half walk to Shoop's house. She had been off an hour by her calculations. She began to walk again. The terrain had become hilly. Spying an exceptionally large hill, Kim decided to go to the top of it. Maybe from there she could see for miles and miles. Maybe she could see the forest she was looking for. She began the challenging climb. Reaching the top, she discovered that she was on the edge of a cliff. Kim took in the breath-taking view, thinking. *I can see the whole world from here*. Looking down. There was a small forest and a thin wisp of smoke coming from the center. Shoop's house.

CRACK. A stick broke under Manon's foot as she moved towards Kim. Knife in hand, her eyes burning holes into Kim, she advanced.

"YOU? YOU!" Kim turned and froze.

Manon threw a knife at Kim's feet. "Let's make this a fair fight, shall we?"

Kim slowly picked up the knife. Her back was to the cliff. Nowhere to go.

Manon stepped forward swinging her knife from right to left and then back from left to right. Kim backed up and looked down behind her. It was a dizzying drop.

Manon stepped in closer, swinging her knife again from right to left and cutting Kim's shirt open. She sliced a thin, jagged cut on her stomach. Warm blood began to flow, reddening Kim's shirt.

Kim thrust her knife back at Manon. She backed her up. Manon punched Kim's jaw with her left hand, spinning Kim to her left.

Both girls stabbed with their knives and stopped the knives with their free hand before either blade connected. Clutching each other, they stared into the other's eyes. Surprising Manon, Kim threw her head onto Manon's face. Crack, her nose crunched, and blood began to drip into Manon's mouth.

Manon backed away, spitting blood. "You bitch!" she screamed.

Circling, they clenched again. Manon's back was now at the edge of the cliff. Kim stepped away and threw a punch, connecting on Manon's broken nose.

Manon swung her knife from side to side, not close enough to connect.

Kim faced Manon. Eying her carefully, she began flipping her knife from hand to hand. First in the right, then in the left, and back again. Manon was mesmerized by the knife's movement. Without warning, Kim punched straight to the face again. Manon stumbled back, dangerously close to the cliff's edge.

Manon swung her knife, but Kim was ready, catching her wrist with her free hand. There was a pause. Then Kim plunged her knife into Manon's side.

Manon gasped. Stepping back, there was nothing but air. With flailing arms and legs, she went down. Desperate, she grabbed the edge of the cliff as loose rocks scattered and fell. She tried to get a better grip. No Good. Panic!

Then two hands grabbed Manon's left wrist. Kim pulled Manon to safety at the edge of the cliff. It might have been the broken nose or the knife wound, but Manon looked up at Kim and passed out. Blackness.

CHAPTER 31

SHOOP'S HOUSE

Dan Shoop was splitting wood outside of his cabin that afternoon. Hearing some noise behind him, he turned to see a young woman stagger into the clearing around his home. A blonde-haired girl was carrying another girl with a fireman's carry. The girl being carried looked to be a bloody mess. Sitting Manon on the front steps of the cabin. Kim turned. "Sir, could you help us? Please!"

Picking Manon up, Dan carried her inside. "Come, come follow me." Laying Manon down on the bed, he began checking all her injuries. Looking at Kim, he said "Your friend's nose will heal. But the wound on her side looks awfully bad." Dan began to work, barking orders at Kim. "Boil some water first, then go into that cabinet and get a sheet. Cut the sheet up, we'll use it for gauze. Open that cabinet to your left. Yes, that's it! See the green bottle? Give me one of those pills. It will help her sleep and take away some of the pain." Dan worked on Manon until he was satisfied that she was going to be okay. Kim stood by, watching the man, and admiring his skills.

Dan had already fixed stew for dinner, and had Kim join him. Kim sat silent, afraid to talk or even make eye contact. *Would he discover why she was really here?*

Dan Shoop was a quiet man by nature. So, conversation was easy to avoid for Kim. He kept checking in on Manon.

Kim asked, "Will she be able to travel back to town tomorrow?"

"Maybe." Came the reply, "Depends on tonight's rest. She's lost a lot of blood. I don't think there's any damage to an organ. The only real problem would be infection. You really need to get her back to town. Doc Klingaman will need to see her as soon as possible."

Kim sat down by the fire and began to stare at the flames. *Had Lexa or Talon sent Manon to kill her.* A chill ran down her spine and she shuddered.

Dan looked over, "Why were you out here?"

Kim kept staring at the fire. *The interrogation begins,* she thought. "I just wanted to explore and see what was west of town. I'm new to the town. I'm staying with Grandma Miller.

Dan chuckled, "She's been around town forever."

Kim was relieved he seemed to buy her lame excuse. She began to study the vast number of books on the bookshelves. Hundreds and hundreds of them. She wanted one book. It would be an impossible task finding one book out of hundreds.

The next morning Manon opened her eyes to see a man checking out her wounds. She jerked away.

"It's okay Manon, he's helping us." Kim said looking down on her. Manon's eyes scanned the cabin and all the books, finally stopping to look at Kim. Kim smiled. Manon turned away, hurting, and confused.

"Can you sit up?" Dan asked.

Slowly, Manon sat up. She was feeling a little weak.

"Now try standing and walking around the cabin." Dan directed.

Gingerly, she stood up. She felt dizzy. Taking a deep breath, she took a wobbly step. Eventually, she made a trip around the cabin.

Dan looked at Kim, "Well, let's get some food in her and then we'll see if you can get her back to town. Kim nodded as she and Manon sat down at the kitchen table. The three sat in silence as they ate their breakfast. Kim's eyes kept scouting for the magic book. No clue.

Manon, on the other hand, was overwhelmed. Kim had saved her. Saved her life.

Dan sat absorbed in what he had been researching. Looking over at Kim, he said "You look familiar to me."

Kim shook her head, "Don't think so. Like I said, I'm new in town."

Finishing up breakfast, the girls packed up. Kim turned to Dan. "I better get this one back to town, like you said."

"Quite right, be careful out there. There are some bad people out and about."

The girls waved goodbye and Kim was surprised to hear Manon say, "Nothing will happen to her. I owe her my life."

CHAPTER 32

KIM AND MANON RETURN TO MUDDVILLE

Kim and Manon slowly walked into town that afternoon. They had not talked much as they made their way through the countryside. Manon had lost a lot of blood, and her broken nose made it hard to breathe. Kim's mind was far away, thinking about the book and her brother. She must save her brother, that was the most important thing on her mind. Manon too was deep in thought. *What would she tell Talon?*

The two finally reached Grandma Miller's house and Kim introduced Manon to the sweet old lady. Looking at Manon, Grandma said "You need to rest. Kim go get Doc Klingaman. His office is down near the high school."

At the same time both girls said, "Yes Ma'am."

Instantly Grandma became a caregiver, fixing up a place

for Manon and making her comfortable. Doc Klingaman arrived and nodded at Grandma. He began cleaning the wound and putting on new bandages. He looked at Manon. "The more you rest the better you'll be. The more you move around the more damage to yourself you'll cause. By the way how did this happen?"

Both girls looked at each other, then back to the doctor. Kim shrugged "Just an accident."

The doctor gave her a puzzled look, standing up as he bid farewell to Grandma Miller.

On the other side of town, Sid and Brucie approached a secluded house on the edge of Muddville. Sid knocked on the door before entering. "Cody?"

"I'm here." Cody turned around. He had been sitting by a window, watching the outside world. Sid sat down beside Cody as Brucie remained standing. Brucie blurted out. "This guy is from the Collective. How do you know he didn't kill my parents?"

Cody spoke, "I didn't. I've never hurt anyone."

Brucie just glared back.

Sid continued, "Well, we brought you some food." He began to examine the damaged shoulder. "Seems like it's healing ok. How do you feel about staying here a little longer?"

Cody muttered, "Like I have a choice?"

Sid and Brucie left the house and headed back to the office,

Back at Dan Shoop's house, Dan was packing up his backpack. Putting in his book 'The History of the World' he took off for town. Thinking about the women that had found his house. *There was nowhere safe for him.* Sid was his only hope. So, he headed to Muddville to find Sid. Entering town, he stopped by the bakery. Walking into the shop, he sat his backpack down just as the baker came from the back.

"So sorry to hear about your job, Dan. How about coffee on the house?"

"Sure," Dan said sadly. "Not sure where I go from here."

Suddenly, the baker screamed, "STOP! STOP! Dan turned as the shop door slammed. "That boy took your bag!" Dan ran to the door and looked up and down the street. Nothing. His book was gone. His life was gone.

At the same time, Sid and Brucie reach Sid's old office. Sid began wondering what he was going to do with the printing press. Brucie asked if he could go out and walk around town. "Sure. Now look, I know you don't trust Cody much, but you can't tell anyone."

"I know." Brucie waved goodbye. Leaving the office, he headed down a back alley. Maybe he'd head towards the school yard and see if anybody was out playing. He stopped in his tracks when he saw Koz hiding in a dark area behind some trash barrels. Brucie stepped back, just out of sight. Koz stood up slowly. His hands were clutching a backpack. Gradually, he began walking towards Brucie's hiding place. Looking in all directions, he began to move faster and then started an all-out sprint.

Brucie stuck his foot out. WHAM! Koz hit the ground. The backpack hit the ground as well. The top was flung open, allowing the book to slide out in the dirt. Title up, it read 'The History of the World.'

"Gotcha!" Brucie cackled, scooping up the book. He sprinted back to Sid with Koz in hot pursuit, whining, "It's mine. It's mine." Busting in the front door of the office, Sid was startled. "Look what I have." Brucie handed the book to Sid.

Koz stood there panting, "It's mine! He stole it from me!"

The door opened suddenly. There was Sheriff James along with Dan and the baker. Looking down at Koz, the Sheriff blocked the doorway. "No, I believe you stole it from Mr. Shoop here."

Koz began to stammer. Looking around, he had no escape.

The Sheriff growled, "Look here I've had enough trouble from you Keys boys. If I catch any of you in town, I will throw you in jail. Got it? Now git." The Sheriff stepped into Sid's office, holding the door open.

Koz saw the doorway open and darted out. Meanwhile, Dan was looking over his book. It seemed no worse for wear.

Dan said, "Thanks for your help Sheriff."

The Sheriff turn to leave. "Just doing my job."

Dan turned back to Sid and Brucie. The three sat down. Looking at Brucie, he said "Thank you." Brucie was beaming. "I have to hide this book. I have an idea, but I need your help. I want you to hide it for me, Brucie. People are watching me. They won't be watching you." Leaning over, Dan whispered in Brucie's ear. "Here's where." Brucie nodded and smiled.

Shoop

CHAPTER 33

THE LIBRARY

Dan Shoop had had a full day. After the excitement of losing his book in the morning, he had done some grocery shopping. He didn't buy a lot, just some food for the day. He stayed around town waiting for the sun to set. He was walking down the street, thinking about his options. *Home was a good bit away. Priorities: research or clean out my classroom? What he needed in the classroom was relatively safe. Library, it was.* He glanced towards the library. *No one in sight. Was his mind playing tricks on him?*

The library door made a creaking sound as he opened it. No one was there. The library had been shut down a few days ago by a new ordinance from the Town Council. Peering around, his eyes became accustomed to the room's dim lighting. Moonlight shining through a few windows gave Dan enough light to see. Moving slowly to the back section of the library, he found his favorite section, the oldest books. Checking titles, he found the one he wanted. Snuggling down under a window he opened his book and began to read with the moonlight illuminating the pages. In minutes he became engrossed in the book. Time ticked on through the night. Suddenly, a book hit the floor at the other end of the building.

"Shhhh, You FOOL! Look! Set the fire and get out of here. I'll meet you later!" came a voice.

Dan strained to see. A black silhouette with a hood. Dan froze. Scooting back into the darkest shadows behind some bookshelves, he waited. Smoke. Footsteps at the doorway. The door creaked open and then shut. Silence. More smoke. Then Dan saw the fire spreading. *There was a back door to this place if he could only find it. Must move quickly! Getting hard to breath! There the door is. Just in time.* Dan opened the door and took a deep breath of fresh air. Trying to stay in the shadows, he moved away from the building. Flames were engulfing it. Alarms were ringing. Dan stood for a second watching the flames eat all those wonderful books. Panicky. *They're here! They're too close. Can't go to the school. I must try to get home.* Shoop saw Sid run up as the townspeople came running. Jake Allen was directing the attack on the fire. "No! No! Don't worry about the library, concentrate on keeping the fire from spreading to other buildings."

Sid came up to Dan, "You okay?"

Dan stammered, "I saw them. They are destroying the written word. Got to go back to my house and collect some things. Did Brucie hide my book?"

Sid grinned, "Yep, he didn't even tell me where he hid it."

Desperate, Dan turned to go, "If I make it back, I hope I can count on you for help." Turning, Dan began to run.

Sid yelled after him. "Count on it." He watched his friend run off.

As the flames illuminated Dan running, no one noticed a shadow following him.

Sid Finch stood and watched the old town library go up in flames. It would have made a good story for the newspaper. Dan had said the Collective was here, and sure enough it was true. Dan was a target, that was clear.

But am I?

A NEW TEAM

The Library

CHAPTER 34

THE SILENCER AND TALON TEAM UP

Talon stood on the outskirts of town watching the fire. She was surrounded by her people. The fire exploded, lighting up the night sky. There. She pointed. "The smaller man there talking to the long-haired man. See him? That's the guy that has the book we want. Alice, go follow him and see where he goes."

Alice sprinted off in the dark after Dan Shoop.

Turning to Jesse and Frank, "Let's get back to camp."

Sid Finch watched the fire a little longer and then turned and headed back to the house where he had told Brucie to go for the night.

Alice kept her distance trailing Dan Shoop. It took over two hours in the dark. The man kept doubling back on his trail and even at times walked in a stream to lose anyone following him. Dan was so fearful of the Collective by now that any sound made him jump. Alice, on the other hand, was very patient and was rewarded by seeing the man finally enter his cabin. She waited in the forest for some time to make sure the man was in for good. Once convinced that the man was in for the night, Alice turned and left for her own camp.

Meanwhile, back at the woods, Talon and the guys entered their own camp. Turning to Frank, "It's been a big day. I'm hungry. Fix some of that deer meat you and Jesse shot the other day. Frank started a fire and began to cook. Putting the meat on a spit, he began to turn it.

Just then Talon saw a silhouette walking towards them through the trees. She stood up as Jesse stepped forward. "Who goes there?"

"Calm down." Came the reply. She stared in surprise as Bart Archer walked into camp. "You didn't have to fix dinner for me." He smirked at Talon.

"What the hell are you doing here?" She barked.

Archer laughed. "I've hired a couple of local boys. They are good trackers. They have come in useful lately. I saw the fire. Was that your work?"

Jesse and Frank turned back to the fire and their cooking as Archer motioned Talon. "Let's go somewhere we can talk in private."

Talon said, "Lead the way." *No way do I turn my back on this guy, she thought.*

The Silencer found a spot out of earshot, where he could watch the men and talk to Talon. He began his pitch. "You and that Schneider girl are after a History book."

Talon nodded.

Archer continued. "The Controller has asked you to

destroy it. But what if that book could be the key to taking over the Collective? Not only that, but this outside world as well!"

Talon's interest was piqued. "What are you saying?"

"My plan," said Archer, looking around "is to get that book. I found out that there are really two books. One here and another with a man headed out west. If someone... If we were to possess both books, we could take out the Controller. You get the book that is here. I will go track down that other man and the second book."

Talon looked at Archer with a twinkle in her eyes. "You are proposing a partnership?"

"Yes." Archer looked back at the camp. "I know that you consider those two the most loyal. The more people we have in on this, the trickier it gets."

Talon straightened. "They are my best. I trust them."

Archer laughed, "I know, I know. Those two, their family has been with the Collective since the beginning. They are true blood Collective. But the two girls with you are rejects. Where are they?"

"Off on a mission." Talon said. "What's wrong with Alice and Manon?"

They were abandoned out here as young children. My men brought them into the Collective and raised them. You can't trust any outsider. I don't care who they are. They are simply different from us, not true Collective. Get rid of them or the deal is off." Archer held out his hand. "Deal?"

Talon paused, thinking about the girls. "Deal." And they shook hands.

CHAPTER 35

DAN SHOOP'S HOME

Waking up early, before anyone in the house, Manon left Grandma Miller's. Heading out of town. She headed towards Talon's camp as she worked her way through the woods.

"Hey, Manon!" Alice came skipping up, startling Manon. Grinning, "I've been scouting a man for Talon. You look a little beat up! What happened?" Manon shrugged and walked on towards the camp in silence. Her wound made it hard to breathe without some pain. She would need a good two weeks for this to heal. That is what the doctor had said.

The two walked into camp as Talon stood up. "Where did the man go?" Alice picked up a stick and drew a map in the dirt. "There." And she pointed at a spot."

"And the book?" Talon asked.

"You didn't say get the book." Alice cried out, seeing that Talon was obviously mad.

Talon turned her wrath towards Manon, "You, did you kill her?"

Manon's head dropped, "She got away."

"FOOLS, You're both fools!" Talon screamed. *She had to act furious to pull this off. Convince all of them that what she was about to do was real.* Get out. I want nothing to do with the pair of you. You are dead to me! Get out! Get out NOW!"

Manon straightened, her hand clutching her knife. Glaring at Talon, "You fucking, backstabbing bitch! Come on Alice, we're not welcome here." Talon's hand was on her own knife as were Frank's and Jesse's. Both stood up ready for a fight. Manon knew it would be death if she challenged Talon. Slowly she and Alice backed away. Alice seemed shaken by the events.

Talon screamed after them, "You failed your missions and then threatened me. How dare you. I'll kill you if I ever see you again."

Manon grabbed Alice by the arm, pulling her they began to run.

Jesse looked at Talon. "Want me to go after them?"

Talon sat down by the fire. "No, let them go."

Kim awoke the next morning. Manon was nowhere to be seen. The whole town was buzzing about the library fire. Eating her breakfast, she thought that it must be Talon's work. "Grandma, I'm going out to Dan's house again."

Grandma smiled. "Okay, be careful." Finishing her juice, Kim left the house on a mission. *Get back to Dan's house and find the books and then find Cody, in that order. What would Dad do?* He would save Cody first.

At that very moment, Manon and Alice ran into town.

Manon led Alice to Grandma's house just as Kim was exiting the back door. Kim stopped, staring at Manon. Alice pulled back, looking at Kim in horror.

Manon gasped, short of breath. Talon cut us loose. She wants to kill us. She is headed back to that cabin to get the book."

Alice was stunned, "How did you know about the cabin?"

Manon waved her off. "I'll tell you later."

Kim looked at Manon, "Then I better go and see if I can beat her there. I need you to follow a man named Sid Finch. He has a boy named Brucie with him. Oh, and there is a kid that has been hanging around town. His name is Koz Keys. People say he has been hanging around strange people. Watch out for him."

"Can we stay here?" asked Manon.

Kim smiled, "I'm sure Grandma will let you. She will probably make you eat breakfast."

Alice grunted, "Why are we working for her now?"

Manon quickly answered, "Alice, I owe her my life."

Kim looked at Alice, "Are you okay with that?"

Alice stepped close to Manon. "Where she goes, I go."

Kim turned "I'm off. See you later."

She walked west along that dirty road. One farm field became another. Some had corn and some fields just had weeds. Kim spotted a man, but when she got close to him, the man was only made of straw.

Along the way she met a farmer. Stopping to talk briefly, she moved on. He was an older man covered in dirt from the fields, wearing a faded blue pair of overalls.

After walking an hour or so to clear her head, Kim saw the big hill and the forest. The big grove of trees was beautiful. *Dan's house in that grove was a nice place to live*, thought Kim.

Entering the forest her heart began to race. She walked into the dark and coolness of the trees. Once there, she had to pause to let her eyes adjust. She had forgotten how far she had carried Manon on her back. Kim walked into the shadowy tree cover, moving forward slowly. Suddenly, she was flat on her face. *Dumb me*, she thought! A tree branch had tripped her up. Brushing herself off, she continued forward. She had forgotten how deep in the woods Dan's cabin was.

A scream! A man's scream echoed in the woods. Kim turned towards the noise. Slowly moving, closer and closer. Silence. As Kim took a few more steps she saw a fire. Ducking behind a tree she watched. Talon and her two men stood over a pile of books. Talon held on to a book with a blue spine. Jesse and Frank were burning the rest of the books. Time passed and the fire began to die down. Kim waited. *How had Talon found this place? She cannot know I am here. Talon must hate me! She has destroyed all of Dan's books and taken the book I want. I am a failure.* She dared not move.

Flames turned to coals as Talon looked at her men. "We're heading back to the school to check the classroom. I want to check it over one more time." As they moved off through the woods, Kim moved in to take a closer look. She entered the clearing where Dan's cabin was positioned to one side. In front of the cabin were the coals of Talon's fire.

Slowly opening the door to the cabin, Kim found Dan laying in a pool of blood. "No, no. no." Kim rushed to the body. He groaned and looked up at her. "At least you're not dead." Kim said.

A feeble, "Close enough," said the man.

Trying to bandage some of his wounds she kind of propped him up in the bed in the corner. Kim shook her head, "You're a mess! You've lost a lot of blood."

"No time for me, you've got to catch them. You must get to my classroom before they do!" Shoop stopped. Looking into Kim's eyes, he smiled. "You're Kelly's sister, aren't you?" Kim nodded. "Look" he continued. "There were two volumes and two books to each set. That lady took the set with the blue spine. They are fake. The real books have a red spine. Half of the other set is safe with a friend, but..." Shoop began to drift away. Kim shook him. "Listen to me! The last and most important book is in my classroom. Forget about me, save my book!" Shoop's eyes wavered, then focused one last time. "Hurry! Go! Go!" He waved her towards the door. Kim began to cry. She walked to the door. Wiping her eyes, she tightened her backpack. Time to use her trail running training.

Kim dashed through the forest. Talon had failed, and she had hope. Why was this book so important that Shoop would give his life for it? She pushed forward. *Could she beat Talon to the classroom?*

It is me or Talon!

CHAPTER 36

MANON GOES HUNTING

Moments after Kim left, Manon and Alice entered the house and talked to Grandma Miller. Sure enough, Grandma insisted on fixing breakfast for the pair. After filling their bellies, they politely excused themselves, dodging a myriad of questions.

Slowly they began walking through town. Alice was getting used to this newfound freedom. Peeking in the newspaper office; the sign read 'CLOSED' but the door stood open. It looked like the owner was cleaning things up inside with the assistance of a young boy. Manon spied a sign on a counter reading 'Sid Finch.' She had found her first target. About to leave, Manon heard the boy ask the man "I wonder if Koz will get the guts to come back into town?"

Waiting just out of sight, Manon listened intently. She heard the reply. "He might. I do not know. I've heard that those Keys boys live out east of town in the woods."

Manon and Alice moved off down the street. "Where too now?" Alice asked.

"East, didn't you hear the man?" Manon turned, looking at Alice.

Alice frowned, "More work for Kim?"

Manon began to walk east, "I told you, I owe Kim a debt. I like it out here, don't you? We might even find a home." Alice followed Manon in silence.

They traveled out of town, heading east. It was lucky they had done so much scouting for Talon. They walked an hour before they found any signs of life. There were voices in the distance every now and then. The two girls slowed and went into stealth mode. Manon froze at the next words she heard. "Hey Koz, get some water for the man."

Crawling forward, Manon saw a cabin. Two young men were talking to....

WHAT? The Silencer! Manon lay ever so still behind a tree. One false move could alert the most dangerous man in the Collective. What was he doing out here? Listening intently, she overheard his next words.

The Silencer began. "I want you two to take me west and track down that Indian Billy."

Tod Keys quizzed, "The Indian, what's he got to do with anything?"

The Silencer turned, looking around as Manon ducked her head. "He's got a book I want. Can you track him?"

The brothers looked at each other. "Sure, that's what we do best."

"We leave tomorrow morning. Be ready."

Manon watched as the Silencer turned and left. She decided to stay put for a while. She did not want to cross paths with the Silencer. Let him get clear of the area before she and Alice went back to town. *Were Talon and the Silencer working together?* Manon wondered. *Nobody in the world could stop them if they were.*

The boy came out of the house with the glass of water. "Where did he go?"

The older brother began to laugh, "Guess he wasn't thirsty." Tod looked at Jay and then Koz. "You know, if that book is such a big deal, if we could get it, we could be rich. Koz's eyes widened. Sheriff James or not, he had to go back into town.

CHAPTER 37

THE HIDDEN TREASURE

Once away from Shoop's cabin and the woods, Kim began to run. Past the old farmer, she raced down the road. Bugs were flying all over the place. She had not noticed them on her trip to the forest. Could she make it in time? As she entered the outskirts of town, she had seen no sign of Talon. *Was she behind or ahead?* Making her way to the school, she wondered where to start this search, stopping at the entrance to catch her breath. Opening the main doors of the school, Kim spotted a tall, skinny man sweeping the floor, "Sir could you tell me where Mr. Shoop's room is?"

"Everyone wants to know today. The man gets fired and now all the world wants to know where his room is. Second floor, first door on the right. Just like I told the others," the man answered disgustedly. "Now leave me alone before I get fired myself."

Others? Was Talon here? Kim moved off towards the

stairwell, slowly moving up stairs. No sign of Talon. First door on the right. Kim paused. Slowly opening the door. She peered inside. Dark, but the sunlight from the windows lit up the room. Stepping inside. *A mess. Talon or her men had been here.* The desks were pushed all over the place. Shoop's desk was upside down. The desk drawers were pulled and thrown aside. Kim searched around. Nothing. Did they get the book? *She was going to fail.* Still, with some determination, Kim began to study the wall areas that had not been searched. *Did Dan have a hiding place?* Turning on the lights to get a better view of everything, she became aware of a shadow on the floor. Suddenly looking up, she saw a darkened rectangle in the ceiling light. *What is that?* Pulling a desk over, she climbed up and stood on her toes. Barely reaching the tile above, it was a struggle to move it as it had some weight. As she shoved the tile off to one side, something moved. Stretching as far as she could, her fingertips felt in the ceiling tile. *A BOOK!* Gingerly inching it to the edge, she worked the book downward. *It had a red spine. Shoop's book. Hurray!* Setting the book down on the desk, Kim climbed down. Now what? Who do I tell? Kim studied the book, titled 'The Age of Technology and the Collective.' "I did it!" She laughed.

"No, silly little girl, I did it! The book is mine! Hand it over." Talon stalked into the room snarling.

Meanwhile, Brucie was playing catch with another boy out in front of the school. He had hidden Dan's book in the teacher's classroom, just as he had been told. Watching the school building as he played catch, he saw Talon enter the school. Tossing the ball back to his friend he said, "Sorry I have to go." He began to walk towards the school, trembling with fear. This was the woman that had killed his parents. There was hatred for the woman and that drove him on. He picked up a rock just in case she attacked him. Talon had not come back. Then Brucie saw a blonde-haired girl enter the school and he followed her in. Creeping up the stairs to Dan's classroom, he heard yelling. Peering in the doorway, he saw the two women. He threw the rock as hard as he could.

"No, it's mine!" Kim protested

The two began to circle the desk with the book in between them. Kim's eyes followed Talon's every move. Talon placed her hand on her knife. "I will enjoy this. I am going to rip you apart." They continued circling the desk. Kim's hand inched towards her own knife. She tried reasoning with the Talon. "I found it! I'm taking it back to the Collective."

"Not a chance."

Their eyes met. Time stood still. CRASH!

Brucie's rock hit the window. Shattering it into pieces. Both women turned to look at the broken glass and that is when a pair of hands grabbed the book. Brucie lifted the book up and sprinted off. Turning, both women ran to the doorway. Meeting in the doorway at the same time they collided. Talon grabbed Kim and threw her back into the room full of desks. "That little bastard!" Talon screamed.

Brucie made it down to the front door and into the street. Talon followed, but he soon lost her in the back alleyways. Talon fumed. *I'll find him!* She watched the town from a hiding place that Koz had told her about. It was the best place to watch everyone.

Kim left the school. *Where did that little boy go?* She

began to search the back alleys, making her way towards Pat's. At the same time Brucie was racing on another route towards Sid's old office. Sid would know what to do. A block away. Just ten more steps. A foot sticks out and Brucie goes flying. The book skidded into the dirt. A cackle and Koz appears. "Got ya back, reject," he said, reaching down to grab the book. As his hand closed in, a foot stepped on Koz's hand.

"Not so fast kid," said Sid.

Koz screamed in pain, whining, "Finders keepers."

Keeping his foot on Koz's hand, Sid said. "No way, it's ours now!"

Koz changed his tactics, "Well, I know someone who will pay you good money for it. We can split the money."

Sid laughed, "Good try, no deal. He took his foot off Koz's hand. "Run off now before I step on you again." Koz moved off sullenly. Brucie picked himself up and stuck his tongue out at Koz. "Thanks Sid, I think that book is more important than Mr. Shoop let on."

"I think you're right," smiled Sid.

Kim heard the scream as she rounded the corner. She saw the pair walking down the street. Tailing them for some distance she concocted a plan. Grabbing a piece of scrap paper, she wrote a quick note.

As Kim followed, she heard Sid speak to the boy. "You go out to the house we're staying at and check in on our new friend, Cody. Stay there tonight and I will meet you tomorrow. I'll take care of the book for the time being." They stopped and Kim froze. Close enough to hear the boy say, "Sid, the lady that killed my parents is in town. She wants the book! That could be trouble!"

Sid nodded. "Run off now, we'll be okay." Kim watched the boy leave. She followed Sid into the heart of the town. People were out shopping. The crowd thickened and Kim worked her way closer to Sid. Just as he got bumped by some people, she tucked her note into his pocket. Instantly turning, she pulled her ballcap over her eyes. Gone. Sid felt the tug on his pocket. Turning, he scanned the crowd. Kim was not to be seen. Reaching in his pocket he pulled the note out. The note read: "Meet at Pat's tonight. Info on Dan Shoop." Sid scratched his head. *Is this a trick?* Still, it piqued his interest.

Pat's it is.......

CHAPTER 38

KIM MEETS SID

Kim arrived back at Grandma's house. Meeting Manon and Alice, the girls sat on the back porch discussing the day's events. Kim explained that Sid Finch now had the book and he also had her brother. She had a meeting with the Finch fellow later that night and hoped to at least steal the book.

Manon explained that the Silencer was going after some guy that had another book. She believed that Talon and the Silencer were working together. That could be really dangerous.

Alice giggled, "If those two get together there's going to be a lot of dead people."

Kim laid out her plan. "If I can get the book tonight, I'm going to head west. I love my brother! If I get the book, I am going to ransom it for my brother's life."

Grandma stuck her head out the door. "Did you say west?"

Kim turned, "Yes I did. I was going to tell you I would be leaving."

Grandma continued, "I used to live out west of here; maybe three days journey. Yes, Dearie. There was an enchanted forest that no one would go into. Most people were afraid to go into it, but not me. I went there all the time. A nice quiet place."

"Thanks Grandma I'll check it out." She turned back to her friends as Grandma shut the door. "Here's the plan; I get the book and go to the enchanted forest. You guys get the other book and meet me there."

Manon nodded. "That means we have to get up early to go out and follow the Keys boys."

They ate dinner that night, all absorbed in what was to happen. Kim wondered. *How can I get the book? Could she get the book and save Cody? It would be just a matter of time before Talon figured out who had the book, if she did not know already. Meet Sid! That's it! No real plan at all.* She sighed. Packing up her things, she told Grandma that she was meeting with a man named Finch tonight. She would be leaving to go west of Muddville and find Grandma's enchanted forest. "You be careful young lady!" Grandma gave her a big hug.

Kim smiled, "I won't forget you. Thanks for everything." They hugged again.

The sun was setting as she walked toward Pat's. *What was this Sid really like?* Kim wondered. Finding the back door to the tavern, she stepped inside and found her old seat. She sat down to wait. As she began to watch the people in the bar, Kim recognized some of them from her last visit. A friendly place where everyone knows your name. *Well, not my name,* she laughed to herself.

Sid entered the tavern, looking around. *He doesn't know who he is looking for,* Kim thought. He went to the bar and got a beer. Turning around, he began to scan the room.

He has the book, Kim realized. Getting up her courage, she raised her hand and gave a small wave. Sid stiffened. Slowly, he moved towards her.

There standing before Kim was one of the very men she had been hunting and the very book that she needed. "Sit down Mr. Finch." The excitement rose in Kim as he set the book on the table. *Could she, should she just flat out grab the book and run?*

Sitting down Sid looked her up and down. "So, you know who I am, but I don't know who you are?"

"I am Kim Schneider," she said proudly.

The waitress came over. "Looks like your glass is empty, Sid. Another? And the lady?" He gave her his mug "Yes, I'll have another. It has been a complicated day. Kim, a beer for you?" Kim hesitated "Sure I'll try one."

"Try?"

Explaining, "Not much beer where I come from."

"That must be a bad place then."

"No, it's really not." Kim defended.

Beers were brought. "I've heard the Schneider name before. But where?" He pulled on his mustache, puzzling. "So, what info do you have on Dan Shoop?"

Kim dropped her head, remembering the dying man. "He's dead. He was killed by the Collective's people."

Sid blew out a big breath. "He kept telling me they were after him." Another big sigh, "Poor guy, his life was this book." Patting the book, he looked at Kim. Are you the Collective?"

Kim changed the subject. "Have you read the book?" Glancing at the book, her eyes remained on it. "Yes and No. I am a speed reader. Rather, a speed understander" he said. Then, signaling for another beer, he turned. "Have you read it?" Kim had seen the title and decided to make up a story of her own. "Well, part of it is about the Collective and the man that runs it; The Controller." Sid was halfway through his third beer and Kim had just taken a sip.

"Fascinating," he continued. "I've heard stories about the Controller. What is he like?"

"Well," Kim thought about her answer. "Let's say he's extremely strict and a devout believer in the Collective's way of life. What's your take on the book?" Kim pried.

Sid yelled at the waitress. "Hey, Brandy! Give me some whiskey." He studied Kim. "You're not drinking much."

She smiled timidly "I am smaller than you are. Besides, it's all so new to me." The beer had a taste that she was not used to. "You were saying about the book?" Kim got a chill down her spine as she looked around. *Was Talon here watching them? Or Lexa?*

"Cheers! Here's to my dead friend." Raising both their glasses, they toasted Dan Shoop. Sid finished his second whiskey, seemingly a little more talkative than when he came in. "The book, or what I read of it, talks about technology. Very confusing stuff. Computers, flash drives as big as your finger. Whiskey!" he yelled. Then, Sid's speech began to slur. "There are these AI programs and mechanical people controlling the world." Sid tried sitting up straight. "I don't think that the people liked being controlled by these so-called robots." Sid's eyes shut then opened but he was somewhere else.

Kim saw how she was going to do it. She could take the book now and cause a scene or ply him with more whiskey and then sneak out. "Tell me about the places you've been to…"

And the stories flowed, along with the whiskey. Kim sat patiently listening about far off places and people. There were wrestling matches and running races. The night grew late and people began to leave the tavern. Soon Kim looked up and they were the last ones left. Silence. She looked over. Sid was slumped over in his chair. The waitress came over.

"Don't worry, Honey. She covered Sid's shoulders with a small blanket. I will take care of him. We'll just let him sleep it off here."

Kim ask politely, "Can I have some paper and something to write with?" Receiving the paper, she wrote a note to Sid and stuffed it in his pocket. Kim turned to leave.

Brandy called out, "Hey wait honey, you forgot this. Handing Shoop's book to Kim. I think you will need this."

Startled, Kim smiled back at Brandy and stored the treasure in her backpack. She was off into the night. Kim had grown to like Sid and his stories. Besides, he had saved Cody. She felt a little sad for the man. All that she wanted was in her grasp now. She controlled her own destiny.

The next morning, a rooster crowed from a nearby farm. Sid sat up. His head was pounding, and his stomach was a mess. Sunlight poured through the open door of the bar. He reached for his book. Gone!

The owner of the bar looked over and laughed at him. "Coffee?"

Sid wobbled a bit standing up. "No, I've got to go meet someone." He staggered out into the street.

The man yelled from the bar, "Hey, check your pocket. She left you a note."

Sid reached into his pocket and stopped to read the note. The note said 'I've been told there's a rather large forest three or four days from here, to the west. Meet me there in one week. I will trade the book for Cody. TELL NO ONE!

Kim

CHAPTER 39

EVERYONE
HEADS WEST

Kim had the book she wanted, and her plan was in place. She got back to the house and packed her things and left, not waking Manon or Alice. Leaving town, she headed west. The first few hours were familiar territory. Passing by Dan Shoop's little forest she thought about the man that had given his life for this book.

A few hours after Kim had left, Manon rousted Alice out of a deep sleep. They packed a few things and left town heading east towards the Kay's cabin. Finding the cabin, they quietly crouched down and laid in the bushes. Hidden from sight they waited for the Silencer to appear. Alice went back to sleep.

A half an hour later the Silencer appeared in front of

the Keys' cabin. Tod and Jay came out and greeted Archer on the front porch.

"Ready?"

"Yes sir!" The boys answered. Turning, they headed off, moving fast.

Manon woke Alice and they began to trail the Silencer, maintaining a great distance so as not to alert him. After half a day, Manon was in unfamiliar territory. The Silencer's group was in a hurry not knowing how far the Indian Billy had gotten ahead of them. Manon had not packed a lot of food. She told Alice, "We're going to have to ration this out and make it last."

The same morning Sid walked very humbly to the house at the edge of town. Thinking, *what will he tell the boys?* He entered the house and Brucie ran to him excitedly, "Where did you hide the book?"

Sitting the boys down, he explained to Cody what Brucie and he had been doing. The book meant nothing to Cody.

Brucie on the other hand was quite upset with Sid. "How could you be so careless and drink so much when you had Dan's book?"

Sid explained the story farther and what he planned to do. Cody became more invested in his plan. "Look, Kim has the book. As far as I can see, we must travel west to that forest and get the book back from her. She wants to trade the book for Cody. I will take Cody to her and she will give us our book; that seems fair to me."

"Don't trust her!" Brucie said.

"What! Of course, we can trust her. Why would we not? Kim is my little sister. Family!"

Brucie's reply came back, "And you guys are the

Collective and we are not." He looked at Sid. "You're dealing with bad people."

Cody protested. "The political leaders might be bad, but the rest of the people in the Collective are just like you. Kim and I are just like you."

Sid ended the debate. "Look, we're going. I've already decided. Pack your things. We head out in an hour. It's a grand adventure Brucie, and you are part of it." The pep talk was more for Sid than for Brucie.

Kim had gained a half a day's lead on Sid and the boys and was moving at a comfortable pace.

CHAPTER 40

THE WESTWARD TRIP CONTINUES

Sid had purchased the necessary supplies for the trip. Blankets, dried food, canteens for water. A tent in case it rained. They each had backpacks. Sid carried the heaviest. Brucie had traveled with his parents while his dad had told stories to make money for the family. But he had never been out of the surrounding territory. Cody was also inexperienced in traveling great distances on foot. His mind alternated between the excitement of seeing his sister and the lows of memories of the battle.

Sid explained as he tightened Brucie's belt around his waist. "You want the weight of the pack to be carried by your waist not your shoulders."

Traveling west for a day, they made their first camp before sunset. Sid was a great storyteller and regaled the boys with many adventures. This made the first day go fast. Sid picked a spot to pitch their camp. A stream was nearby so they could get water. Some tall trees stood some hundred yards away from their camp. They could hang their food up high on a big branch so animals could not get to it in the middle of the night.

Watching the fire, Cody asked "When are we going to get there?"

Sid replied, "Two more days to walk. Then, probably three days after that waiting for our meeting with Kim. We'll have to find that forest she talked about."

Brucie looked up and asked, "How'd that Billy guy get in and out of the Collective?"

Cody answered the question. "The people's bodies are stored in massive buildings. The bodies are laying on beds with tubes hooked to them to feed them and to keep them healthy. There is a cap on each person's head with wires that connect their minds to the Collective. The combination of their thoughts creates the Collective's virtual world. I was part of the security force that worked on the outside of those buildings to help protect the bodies. Mostly a boring job. We worked five days on the outside and then went back into the Collective for ten."

Sid finished the story. "Dan Shoop told me that Billy snuck into one of those buildings. He watched the security guys as they changed shifts. So, one day he found an empty bed and hooked himself up. The hard part was for him to come back out. He had to wake himself up on his own. I suppose it would be like trying to wake up in the middle of a bad dream."

Cody then added, "Scientists in the Collective monitor

all thoughts of the people. They knew that Billy was there at times, but he never got caught."

Sid looked around. "Time for bed, boys."

Brucie and Cody laid in their blankets and looked at the stars.

Looking at the stars herself, Kim had made good time and was six hours ahead of the boys. She also sat at her camp and enjoyed the night sky. She wondered about her brother. *What was Manon doing?*

The Silencer and his team were moving fast. One brother would run ahead and scout for signs and then come back and trade places with the other brother. They saw very few people. Most of the people out here avoided strangers. Mothers would shoo their children inside their homes as the boy's passed by. They made camp after sunset and woke before sunrise.

Manon and Alice did not have the comfort of a fire. It would signal the Silencer that someone was following him. She and Alice slept together using their own body heat to warm themselves.

Day two was pretty much the same for all parties. The Silencer maintained a hard pace. Manon and Alice kept their distance for the time being. Sid and the boys continued their hike but with a little less storytelling. Brucie needed more rest stops. This gave Kim and even bigger lead. *A long stretch of road will teach you more about yourself than one hundred years of quiet introspection.*

That night over the campfire Brucie asked, "Who's Kelly?"

"Well," Sid said, "Kelly is Cody's older sister and Kim is his baby sister. Kelly was friends with Billy and Dan Shoop. Dan told me that she is headed way out west to see some big ocean."

Cody hung his head. "I don't remember her much. Just a face. They tried to erase her from all our minds."

Sid continued, "This is from Dan, mind you. Kelly came out of the Collective with Billy. After a while she missed her family and went back inside the Collective. She was caught and tortured. Billy and some friends from Muddville rescued her. There lies the whole problem. Now the Collective knows about us and we know about them." Chuckling ruefully, he said "Man, this would be a great newspaper story."

Brucie piped in, "And my Dad could have made a great yarn to tell."

Day three was overcast for Sid and the boys as they traveled along. Kim was now close to where she wanted to be, and asked some woman doing laundry where the enchanted forest was. There was no reply, the woman only pointed a finger in the direction.

The Silencer's path was way north of Sid and the boys. He had not wasted time by taking breaks. They hiked north and northwest. Tod Keys made it back from his scouting. "I found tracks."

The Silencer slowed down. "We don't want to overrun the man and warn him. Jay, see if you can find him and come back and report."

Jay ran off.

Manon had closed the gap on the Silencer. Cold and hungry, she was glad for the slower pace. She had had to keep pushing Alice to keep up. "I promise you, after this we can find our own home. You are my only family" she said. Always loyal to Manon, Alice kept going without a word. A few hours later they saw one of the boys return and talk to the Silencer. The group stopped early to pitch their camp. Leaving Alice, Manon crept in closer.

Kim had found the enchanted forest and entered it just as it began to rain. The trees protected her from most of the rain.

Sid and the boys were not so lucky. For them, it had begun in the morning with a light rain and by the afternoon it was a downpour.

Manon had snuck in dangerously close to the Silencer's camp. All of Talon's training had paid off.

The Silencer was drawing a map. "He's here. We are here. Tomorrow, I want you guys to circle around way in front of him. Then work your way back towards him. He is a day in front of us, so you must move quickly."

Tod asked. "Do we kill him?"

The Silencer looked over at them. "No! Just scare him back this direction. I'll be waiting."

Tod looked at Jay. "This is easy. This guy has not been moving amazingly fast. Looks like he's been taking his old, sweet time."

Manon crept back to Alice. "We need a plan. Let's be patient and wait. I'll think of something."

Sid Finch

CHAPTER 41

THE INN

Sid looked at the long hill in front of them. Up ahead in the distance, Sid saw a shimmering light. "Hurry boys! We've made it."

It had rained all day. The wind had blustered against the party of adventurers, hitting them square in the face all day. Soaked to the bone, they trudged towards the inn. Water filled their shoes with every step.

"Food?" Brucie looked up at Sid.

"Food, drinks and maybe a warm bed if we play our cards right." Sid patted the boy on the back. Shaking the rain off as he entered the inn, they noticed a fireplace with two or three people sitting around it. The innkeeper looked up. A strong gust of wind pushed the travelers in and slammed the door against the wall.

"Shut the damn door!" one of the customers yelled.

Then, looking square at Sid, he asked "And who might you fellers be?"

Sid puffed out his chest saying, "I am the great Sid Finch, world traveler and the last of the great storytellers. These here are my friends Brucie and Cody. Now who might you be?"

The man grinned, "I am Frank and that is Shawn. He owns the place." He pointed at the man behind the bar. Frank looked to be in his forties. He had shiny black hair that was slicked back. Sid noticed he had a cleft lip that exposed his front teeth.

Looking at Shawn, "Do you have rooms for the night. Can I get a beer? Oh, and can we get some food?" Sid asked. Shawn was a big man with an unshaven face. The light shined bright off his bald head.

"Damn." Shawn grunts, "Too many damn questions. Warm yourselves by the fire and I'll try to answer when I feel like it."

Brucie pulled Cody over by the fire as Sid walked to the bar. *The boy had kind of warmed up to Cody and had been taking care of him. The shock from the battle has run deep.* The man poured Sid a beer. He stood watching the boys. They had stood up well on this trip so far. Shawn left the room as Sid turned his attention to the men in the corner. *Cody had not moved, once seated. More nightmares.* Shawn came back in. "We do have a room, and my wife is digging up what's left of dinner. You got money?"

Turning to Shawn, Sid replied, "I've got money, or we could work it off. We might just be here for a couple of nights."

Shawn smiled for the first time that night. "Work it is. I have lots of it. Done deal." Sid shook hands with the innkeeper and moved over to join the boys.

Half an hour later, Sid's group was warm, and their bellies were full. "See, I told you guys we'd make it and be okay." Sid said.

Frank looked over at Sid. "So, you're a storyteller. The last of the 'Great storytellers.'"

"That's right," Sid replied.

"Well now, let's hear a story."

That is how Sid began his first night of telling stories at the inn. Quite fun, really. He might embellish the facts a little, it would make the story more interesting. All the truths in the world are held in stories. Thinking they might find that amusing, he began to talk about his past. Telling about his wrestling match with the Ohio Valley champion and only losing by a point. Then, he launched into his world travels. "So, you see I'm in Spain one day and…."

Frank cuts in, "Where's that?"

"On the other side of the Ocean!"

"What's that?"

Really, there was no getting through to these people, Sid thought.

Another man said, "Aw, come on Frank, let him talk. Ain't never heard a storyteller before. My Pappy says there used to be a lot of them. Then they kind of died off."

Brucie piped in, "Or they were killed."

Sid said, "Tell you what. Come back tomorrow night and I will tell you a real story. I believe it's time for bed."

Standing up, Sid gave Shawn some money for the food. "We'll be ready to work bright and early tomorrow morning."

Frank and his friends started to leave. "That there story better be really good."

Smiling, Sid headed towards the stairs. "It will be good. Frank, bring more friends."

Two small beds were situated in the room. Cody took one and Sid and Brucie slept in the other. Cody would be tossing and turning all night.

Ahhh, a soft pillow and Sid was out.

The sun winked at Sid and the boys the next morning as they began their day at Shawn's Inn.

CHAPTER 42

THE SILENCER CAPTURES BILLY

Billy sat by his fire, enjoying its warmth. He had taken his time travelling. Once away from Muddville, he had relaxed. Traveling one day and then camping several days in one place. He enjoyed hunting and fishing in this free land. He missed his family, but also loved being one with nature. He was in no hurry and did not feel threatened.

A noise off in the woods drew his attention. He became very alert. Listening for more clues, he slowly packed his things. There was not much to pack as he was traveling fairly light. Other than Dan Shoop's book, there wasn't much weight. He began to move away from the sound he had last heard. It had been northwest of him.

Retracing yesterday's steps, he headed southeast. He moved slowly, pausing every now and then listening.

The Keys brothers spread out, forcing Billy in front of them. They must not let the man past them, or they would be in trouble.

The morning came and went, and Billy became more fearful. Whatever or whoever it was, he was definitely being followed. Billy tried running at one point to see if they could keep up. They did. He tried changing directions, but the trackers always forced him back the same way. As time went on, Tod and Jay became bolder. Billy now knew there were two of them. Stepping into a clearing, he decided to run. But then a man stood up from a campfire.

The Silencer held a pistol in his hand. "Well, well, what have we here?"

Billy froze. Tod and Jay stepped out of the woods behind him. "Sorry Mister." They shoved Billy down by the fire and tied his hands behind his back. Jay grabbed the pack, pulled out the book and handed it to the Silencer. Looking down at the title 'The History of the World.' "This is it boys!"

Billy sat looking at the Silencer in his black uniform. He had failed Dan.

At that very moment Manon and Alice were watching. Whispering, Alice said, "I'm quick! I can run in and grab the book and we'll be gone."

Manon shook her head. "Just wait, it's too risky."

The brothers were looking through Billy's bag to find anything of value.

The Silencer turned towards the boys. "Well, your job is done, and so too your usefulness has ended."

Tod looked up just as the bullet struck him in the head. Jay made it up to his feet, only to meet another fatal bullet. Their bodies fell by the bag. Billy could do nothing but look on. Turning back to Billy, the Silencer said, "I love it when a plan comes together."

Manon looked at Alice. "Breathe, focus, strike."

Alice nodded. Rising slowly, she sprinted at the Silencer while his back was turned.

The Silencer turned in surprise to face his attacker, only to be met with a punch to the face. Grabbing his wrist, she quickly twisted and threw him to the ground. The Silencer tumbled and fell as his gun skidded off into the trees.

Rolling back to his feet, he stood facing his opponent. Alice was lightning quick and sent a crushing kick to the Silencer's jaw.

Manon sprinted to Billy to try to untie him.

Alice charged the Silencer and sent a kick to his body, but he caught her foot and threw a punch to her face. Blood flew. Grinning as though she felt nothing, Alice advanced. She threw a series of punches to his face, driving him backwards.

The Silencer stepped back. He paused, then charged. He drove his shoulder into Alice and knocked her into a nearby tree. This knocked the wind out of her. Before she could react, he plunged a knife into her heart.

Blood poured from Alice's mouth. Her grin was still there as she looked over at Manon. "Sorry."

Manon struggled to untie Billy. She slowly rose to face the Silencer. He turned his attention to Manon, leaving Alice's body as it slid to the ground.

He closed the distance, thrusting the bloody knife at Manon. Two quick kicks to his belly drove him backwards to the ground. The knife flew out of his hand. He rolled back to his feet, facing Manon. They circled each other.

All Billy could do was watch.

The Silencer threw a punch. Manon countered with two upper cuts to his belly and then a smashing shot to his nose. Her combination finished with a kick.

The Silencer countered with a punch of his own.

Manon tried to kick again but he caught her leg and flipped her down to the ground. Getting up to her hands and knees. The Silencer gave her a vicious kick to the midsection, which knocked her back to the ground. She gasped for air as the Silencer circled her. "Baby!" he screamed.

Manon was on her hands and knees now.

The Silencer paused, getting ready to end the fight.

Manon half rose, then with stunning quickness she did a half cartwheel. Instantly she was next to the Silencer. Her hands were at his feet and her back was to him. Locking her feet around his neck she began to squeeze. She let her body weight pull them both to the ground as she continued cutting his air off.

She raised up on one elbow looking at the Silencer.

Gasping for air he rasped, "I'll give you money. I'll give you power."

Manon looked him in the eyes. "You killed my only friend!" With all her strength, she twisted her legs and hips viciously. The stunning combination snapped the Silencer's neck.

The most feared man in the Collective lay dead at Manon's feet.

CHAPTER 43

THE LAST DAY

Sid and the boys had been cutting wood for the inn keeper the first two days of their stay. At night Sid would entertain the locals with stories about the Collective. Each night seemed to draw more and more people to hear his stories.

Tomorrow was the day they were to meet Kim in the forest. Rising early, they loaded a wagon with the wood. Shawn provided them directions to the neighboring farms where they would sell the wood. It was a rather good day in all. Riding, they got to talking. Cody, of course, was excited to see his sister and talked about his family to no end. Brucie, on the other hand, had made good friends with Shawn's kids and had a crush on one of his daughters. Sid was sure Shawn would have none of that. Each farm they visited was nice to the threesome. Buying a rick or two of wood. Always offering a glass of water or a cookie. It took them all day to travel and sell it all. They were always in view of the big dark forest. The families were easy to talk to and told the story of what they called the 'Enchanted Forest.'

The story went something like this: Once upon a time there was an evil ruler. Extremely cruel, he demanded that the people live in his castle. A large group of people entered the castle life. The few that did not want to be controlled left. Fearing the anger of the ruler, they looked for a place to hide. There was nowhere to conceal themselves. Thinking of the dark forest, the people ran to it and began to live deep in the woods.

The Lord and his generals devised a plan to trap the people in the woods. Once caught, they were killed. From that day forward, no one had ever ventured into the woods. The story ended with a warning: the forest is enchanted; haunted by all the poor souls slaughtered that day.

Brucie's eyes widened as he heard the story. Shaking, he said. "And we are going in there?"

"Yes, we are. Cody needs to see his sister and we want the book back." Sid reassured the boy.

"What if the Lady in Black is there?"

Trying to sound brave, Sid said "We'll just have to fight her!"

Brucie shook his head, "None of us is that tough!"

"Now, now boy it is all a story, just like the stories that I tell. We'll be fine." Sid answered.

They arrived back at the inn shortly before dinner time. Sid and the boys cleaned up. Sid put on his best storytelling clothes. Brucie was off playing with Shawn's kids. Cody was sitting by the fire. *What is he thinking about? The stories of the day or his sister? He loves his family. Will the Collective let him back in?* Sid wondered.

Dinner was served. A wonderful roasted chicken.

Shawn's wife was an excellent cook. The clean-up proceeded with everyone helping with chores. Brucie and Cody helped dry the dishes. The bar was cleaned up by Sid and Shawn. They expected a big crowd tonight.

True to form, Frank brought in a lot of people. The inn was rather crowded, and it became hard for Sid to make eye contact with everyone.

Sid began talking about the Collective. Frank asked, "Do they ever come outside anymore?"

So, Sid started telling the story of the battle. "They did a while ago, south of Muddville. The town sheriff is a big man whose name is James. Learning about the attack on his town, he gathered up some of his best hunters and farmers."

Sid's story painted the Sheriff as a brave man and told of the unbelievable sharp shooting skills of the Muddville men. He began to depict it as a real battle with strength and weakness on both sides. The night wore on and he told about those on the right flank and the left flank. The crowd was hooked. Shawn, or someone, had placed drinks in front of Sid and the boys. Sid's throat became dry, and he would talk and then take a drink. Looking down at Brucie, Sid saw he was already asleep. *Strange? Usually he loves any story, but he had had a long day.* Cody seemed rather in a daze. Sid finished the story with the glorious victory of Muddville. The crowd applauded. Feeling rather lightheaded, Sid begged forgiveness and called it a night. Holding Brucie in his arms, he stopped to tell Shawn that he thought they might be moving on tomorrow.

He shook Sid's hand, "Too bad. You are welcome back anytime."

Lying in bed, sleep came fast. Cody and Brucie were out

and soon Sid was slumbering away. After a short time, they were roughly awakened. Sid's hands were tied, and he was gagged. The boys were also bound and gagged. A woman's voice hissed, "Bring them along, we are going to the dark forest to meet our friend." Brucie was shaking. Cody stared wide-eyed at the lady. There was hate in his eyes as he looked at her. She only smiled back at him. "Come along. We have things to do." Grabbing Brucie, she shoved him in front of her. A man took control of Cody and another had Sid in a tight grip. A knife dug into Sid's back.

They travelled quickly in the direction of the dark forest. The lady looked at Sid. "That was sure a whopper, that story you spun last night. You were in rare form, I must say. So rare that you never saw me drug your drinks." Laughing, "I love it when a plan comes together." She jerked Brucie back in line. "Try anything and I'll kill you now."

An hour later they entered the dark forest. It was still before dawn. Some distance away, they could see a small campfire. Cody stiffened. They moved forward. Sid tried to free his hands. Too tight.

At the edge of the campsite, still hidden by the trees, the Lady in Black stopped them. Quietly she said, "Make a sound and you die." Pausing there, Sid realized they were watching Kim. She had been waiting for Sid and the boys all night. Her head drooped as though she might be going to sleep. At that moment, they were suddenly pushed out into the clearing, stumbling on the ground, and falling in a pile. Kim started up.

The Lady in Black stepped forward.

"Time to say goodnight, little girl."

CHAPTER 44

MANON AND BILLY

Manon stood up, looking at the Silencer's body. She gave him a solid kick to make sure he was dead. Turning, she walked over to Billy and cut the ropes that bound him. Then she walked over to Alice and slumped to the ground, hugging her friend's body. She began to sob. Rocking back and forth, she hugged the lifeless body.

Several long minutes later, Manon stood and turned, "My name is Manon." She watched Billy build up the fire. "Kim Schneider sent me to help you."

Billy's eyes widened, "Schneider you say? Kelly's sister is out here?" Looking around he said, "Looks like they left us enough food for dinner. Let's stay here for the night and we'll see what tomorrow brings.

Manon nodded.

She looked down at her side. Blood. The old knife wound must have opened during the fight.

Billy went to his bag and pulled out something. Holding it up to show Manon, he said "This is a plant remedy called yarrow. It will reduce the bleeding." Taking Doc Klingaman's bandage off, he applied the medicine. Then he slowly reapplied the bandage. Looking up at Manon, "Better?" he asked.

Manon said, "Yes."

That night as they watched the fire burn down, Manon explained that Talon had killed Dan Shoop. Talon was still searching for the book that Kim had. Dan had sheltered Manon herself after Kim had saved her life. Kim had found Dan's book at the school, but then lost it to a man named Sid Finch. Finch had also rescued Kim's brother Cody after the battle. Kim had stolen the book back from Sid, and now was going to trade it for her brother.

Billy chuckled. "That book has been all over the place. Where's Talon?"

Manon shrugged, "I'm not sure. I think the Silencer and Talon have teamed up to get the books so they could take over the Collective."

Billy grimly said, "I've seen some of her work." Shaking his head, "A bad, bad, lady. You know, I would like to meet up with Kim and Sid. First thing tomorrow, we should bury these bodies. Then we will try to find that forest you mentioned."

Manon agreed, "Okay, I think I will go to bed now." She was sore from the fight, and the pain of the knife wound made her nauseous. The night was long as thoughts of Alice kept her awake.

CHAPTER 45

THE BATTLE WITH TALON (KIM NARRATES)

Recalling the events of the night, Kim tells her side of the story. She had concocted a plan to save Cody. Finding a place in the woods to set up camp, I began to wait for Finch and the boys. *They might come tonight, but more likely tomorrow.* I sat at my campfire, half asleep. Suddenly three bodies tumbled into the clearing. I saw Cody, Sid and the boy all tied up. Talon stepped into the firelight.

"Time to die, no hard feelings."

Shaken, I stepped back, grabbing my knife. Talon calmly approached me, her knife in hand. With astonishing speed, she closed the distance and thrust the knife at me. Stepping back, I was able to counter her attack. The old familiar practice of sparring came back to me quickly. *Talon's rage and strength would be too hard to attack. I must go on the defensive. Talon seemed to be ready, knowing every thought and move before I made it. How can I escape? She was going to kill me!*

She maneuvered me to where she wanted me; trapped by trees to my right and the fire to my left. Talon began to attack. Circling in a way that limited my movements. I had no place to move. Then came an attack. I tried to block, but it was a weak attempt. A second attack began, as she changed her direction in the very middle of the thrust. Something cold tore my shirt. Pain surged through my right-side ribcage. I jumped back, gritting my teeth, and getting into my best defensive position. Blood dripped down my side. I saw Cody's eyes widen as my white shirt became red.

Talon stepped back, smiling at her result.

Another attack like that would kill me. I was out of options. Maybe attack Talon's face? The next attack came, and I countered with a thrust at her face. My knife came nowhere close, but it did make Talon step back.

"Now. Now. Kim, are you trying to ruin my pretty face?" Talon's face twisted into a savage rage.

The next attack came, and I blocked it. Wait, that wasn't the real attack. The real attack came. Nothing to block it with but my left hand. I grabbed the blade as the knife sliced across my palm. More Pain. Blood flowed.

Back to defense. My hand was all bloody. Twisting one more time at Talon's face.

Use your intuition! My gut told me there had been an opening. My gut reacted to all the hours of training and drills.

No time to think. This is my life. A feeling of calmness washed over me.

I attacked with the same thrust to the face. Talon's counter was better this time. Not going back to defense, I immediately arched forward and thrust a second time over Talon's block. My blade hit home. My knife sunk deep into her neck. Talon's eyes widened in shock. She gasped and crumpled to the ground.

As Talon lay dying, her two men stepped forward. In a flash, Cody stood up and rushed the bigger man. He knocked the breath out of him by ramming him into a tree with his shoulder. The second man ran forward to help.

There was a foot. Brucie had stuck his foot out, tripping the man. Immediately, Sid sat on him.

Weak but happy, I sliced the rope on Cody's bindings. Cody and I hugged. Dizzily, I slumped to the ground.

Cody helped Sid and Brucie with the ropes that tied them. Using the rope, they tied up the two men. Jesse and Frank were quiet, seeing Talon's dead body.

The sun had risen during the fight. Sid attended to my wounds and the boys went looking for water. Sid and Cody recommended that we camped here for a few days so I could recover.

I was so happy to see Cody. He was like a mother hen around me, trying to comfort me and take care of all my needs. I offered Sid the book. "A deal is a deal."

He just smiled at me, but he said nothing.

I was tired and sore from the fight. The day passed quickly as I rested.

That evening Cody was fixing the fire for dinner and

I heard something in the woods. What could it be? Cody heard it too and stood up, as did Sid.

Suddenly Manon and a dark-skinned man walked into the camp.

"Manon!" I screamed, "You're alive!" We hugged, and I held her at a distance. "The Silencer?" Looking around, "Alice?"

"Both dead." Manon dropped her head and began to cry.

CHAPTER 46

RECOVERY

Sid walked over to Billy, introducing himself. The two men shook hands. Dinner that night was a special time for the group. They pieced all the stories together from everyone's point of view. Sid talked about adopting Brucie after his parents were killed. Billy told Cody and Kim about their older sister and the trip she had planned to go and see the big ocean. Manon told about her fight with the Silencer, followed by Kim reliving the fight with Talon. Cody had found himself a seat next to Manon. Every now and then he would lean over and talk to her. Kim smiled at them. She was happy.

The sun was about ready to set. Manon rose and said, "I am going to the edge of the woods and watch the sunset." Slowly, she walked through the trees. Picking a spot of soft grass, she leaned up against a big oak tree. Watching the sun dip below the horizon, she thought about Alice.

The group had decided to sleep late and then walk back to the inn. They would spend one or two nights there. There, each would decide where life led them next.

Kim got up and walked through the trees. Finding Manon, Kim sat down next to her. Tears were running down Manon's face. The two sat in silence for a long, long time.

Manon began to sob. "She was my only friend. I keep thinking if I stare at the sun long enough Alice will be alive."

The sun finished setting and blackness enveloped the world.

Kim put her arm around Manon. "I'm your friend. You are like family to me now. If you ever need anything I'll be there." The two hugged. They stayed a while longer, listening to the crickets. Then, they walked back to camp in silence.

Waking late, the group took their time packing. They headed out towards the inn. It was a good day for a walk. Billy and Sid led the way, pushing Jesse and Frank before them. The two men found they had a lot in common.

Brucie trotted after the Billy and Sid. He was happy to know that his parent's killer had been destroyed.

Kim was next. Her head was filled with confusion about her future. *The books? The Collective? Who did she owe loyalty to?*

Cody and Manon were walking together at the end of the group. Suddenly, Manon blurted out, "Oh! Shut up. I hate it when guys bug the crap out of me."

Cody stopped talking, but he felt Manon's hand sneak into his own hand. He turned and smiled at her.

CHAPTER 47

LIFE AT THE INN

Shawn welcomed the band of adventurers in. The inn was just what Sid had said it was; warm and friendly. The group settled in, as everyone began to think about the future. Jesse and Frank had been locked up in Shawn's barn. They had not decided what to do with them. Maybe they would take them to the Sheriff in Muddville. Maybe the Collective would come after them. That was an unsettling thought for Sid and Billy.

Manon and Cody had gone for a walk. Making it to a small pond down below the inn, they stopped to watch the ducks. Manon looked over at Cody asking, "What do you want from me?"

Cody leaned in and kissed her on the lips. The kiss was just a second, but to Cody it felt like forever. A second later, Manon was back to her old self. Turning and running, she yelled "Race you back."

Cody sprinted after her, laughing all the way back to the inn.

In the meantime, Sid and Billy sat down next to Kim. Sid began "We're all here because of you." Billy place both books in front of Kim. "You are now the keeper of the books. Dan trusted you and so shall we."

Kim gasped, "ME!" Remembering the dying man, she nodded.

Cody, out of breath, stood with Manon by the door. Looking over at Kim, he said, "I can't go back to the Collective. After the battle, I just don't trust them anymore. Sorry, Sis. I think I'm going out west to search for Kelly."

Kim smiled, knowing that was for the best. Her eyes teared up. "I will miss you." Cody put his arm around Kim. "Or you could come with me?" Ignoring the offer for a moment, she looked at Manon.

Manon smiled looking at Cody, "I think I'll tag along with him for a while. Is that okay with you, Cody?"

Cody beamed. "It would be great."

"What about you two?" Kim turned her attention to Sid.

"Not sure. We just might go down to the Ohio valley and find a town that needs a newspaper man, or I could take the boy and explore the world. Brucie and I make a surprisingly good team."

Kim smiled.

Later, everyone gathered around the fireplace, talking about the future. The door to the inn opened. A woman stepped in. She was tall with short purple hair. Looking around she came towards Kim.

She stiffened. "Lexa?"

Shawn looked up, "May I help you?"

Walking over to Kim she said, "No, I'm here to see this young lady."

The whole group stood up, blocking her approach.

"Relax, I just want to talk." Looking around, "Alone! Please."

Kim looked at her friends. "It's okay. Go outside for a few minutes while we talk."

They headed towards the door to go outside. Sid turned. "You need any help, just yell." Kim nodded. Lexa and Kim moved to a corner in the back.

"The future is yours" Lexa began…….

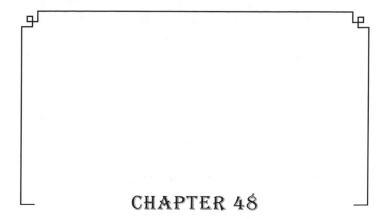

CHAPTER 48

THE FUTURE

Lexa smiled at Kim with her strange little smile, "I'll say it again. The choice of how the future is shaped is yours."

Kim looked at Lexa. "What does the Controller want now?"

"He does not know I am here." She smiled again.

"What about Talon and the Silencer?" Kim asked.

"Both gone, thanks to you." Lexa replied, brushing her hair back.

Kim asked, "Explain to me why you and Talon worked together, I'm just a little curious."

Lexa spoke calmly. "We did not work together. Her purpose was death, as was the Silencer's. My purpose is life." Sitting there looking at Kim, she continued. "You have learned much here. Their way of life. You also know our ways as well. You have grown strong and independent. You may come back to the Collective or stay here; whatever you like. May I ask you one question? What do you think about the people out here?"

Thinking about what she'd experienced, Kim said, "Well, I think you said the right word. Independent. Curious. They want to learn, but not the way we do. They question everything. Whereas we pass the test and question nothing. Look Lexa, can I really go?"

Lexa nodded. "I have what I want. The people here do not know about our world, and the people in the Collective do not know about these people. You are the only one that knows the truth."

Then, looking at Lexa, it dawned on Kim she had one more question. "I heard a story once about a robot controlling the world. I also heard that the people didn't like that much."

Lexa smiled. "Do you have a question in there?"

"Well, are you a robot?" Kim leaned forward, looking at Lexa and studying her face.

"Ah, if I were one of those robots, my first goal would be to protect human life." Lexa smiled, "Hypothetically of course."

Kim laughed. "I suppose you're right. Would there be any other goals?"

She began, "Hypothetically, if I were one of the robots, the goal above protecting an individual's life would be to protect all humanity. And now I am giving you that very job. You see, you can tell either side about the other, or you can keep quiet and they both will live in peace. You also can give the books out and promote the advancement of technology more quickly, or you can wait. If what you say about their curiosity is true, down the road we will have to deal with that anyway."

They sat there in silence, staring at each other.

Lexa added, "So you see, you are the one constant that I will count on. As for myself, I will take the two prisoners you have back to the Collective. Their minds will be wiped of any knowledge of what they have experienced."

Looking at her, Kim questioned, "So you have been the protector all along?"

She smiled, "Only from behind the scenes. I must go. I hope you have a good life." Standing up, she shook Kim's hand.

"Wait, I have one more question." Kim looked at Lexa, "How did you know we were here?"

Lexa stepped to the door. Opening it, the yellow sunlight hit her purple hair. She looked back at Kim. "Grandma Miller has informed me about you every step along the way."

Kim stared after her. "WHAT! Does she work for you?"

Lexa laughed, "or maybe she just likes humanity." As quickly as she had arrived, she was gone.

Kim sat there with a thousand questions swirling in her mind. She was alone and her life was her own. *A new road begins*, she thought. Then she smiled.

The gang came back in. "You okay?"

Kim nodded. Looking down at the books with the red spines. *I am free, and the choice is mine. What do I do with the books?" Where do I go next?*

They had one last glorious dinner together before they parted company. Dinner and stories were shared all around as the fire burned late that night.

CHAPTER 49

BIG PLANS

Manon and Cody packed and left the next day, heading west in the same direction Kelly had gone. Billy had described the map that he had given her and the route that he thought she would take. Kim hugged Manon. "Remember, you are my friend and part of my family." Turning to Cody, they embraced. "Come back someday."

Cody smiled, "I will, and maybe I will bring Kelly with me." Off they went, happy together. Cody had not felt this excited and alive in his whole life. Manon was beginning to think she finally had a family.

Billy stayed on for a while and helped Kim build a cabin in the Enchanted Forest. When the project was done, they had one last dinner together to celebrate. Billy said, "I keep saying this, but I've been away from home too long. I'll leave you to yourself tomorrow. What will you do?" he looked at Kim.

"I don't know." Looking at the two lonely books on her new bookshelf. "I guess I have some reading to do."

Kim and Billy laughed.

Far, far away to the west, Kelly Schneider wiggled her toes in the sand as the ocean water slapped at her shins. The journey had taken her six long months and included many adventures along the way. It was as beautiful as Billy had said it would be. She smiled, wondering how Cody and Kim were.

A few years later, Brucie walked down a street in a town by the Ohio river. Sid and Brucie had started their own newspaper together. He stopped and looked down at a beggar rattling his tin cup. Leaning over looking at the man, he said, "How about you come work for me and my partner at the newspaper?"

The man looked at Brucie, "Why the hell would you do that?"

Brucie grinned, pulling Koz Keys up to his feet. "Cause I want to. What's your real name?"

The reply came "Mark."

Brucie patted Mark on the back, "Well let's see if we can give you a better future." The two headed off towards the center of town. The sun was shining on a new day...

ABOUT THE AUTHOR

Brinton Farrand grew up in Homeplace, Indiana. He attended Carmel High School and Purdue University. His main interests from childhood through college were wrestling and art. After completing his wrestling career at Purdue, he spent the next thirty-two years teaching art and coaching. He evolved over that time from a wrestling coach into an artist. He believes an artist is either ahead of or outside of society, observing people from a unique perspective. He watched the educational system evolve from a community based on the individual students to a system based on data and statistics. Farrand's art classes were free from the control and confinement of this data driven school life. Retired now, he spends every day in his studio drawing and painting. As he pursued variety and creativity, the idea of writing and illustrating a book blossomed. He published his first short story 'The Test Takers' in 2011. 'The Last of the Storytellers' expands on the ideas and characters first met in the short story.

Printed in the United States
By Bookmasters